WHAT IS THE MATTER WITH MARY JANE?

WHAT IS THE MATTER
WITH MARY JANE?

A Cautionary Tale

Daisy Waugh

HEINEMANN : LONDON

William Heinemann Ltd
10 Upper Grosvenor Street, London W1X 9PA
LONDON MELBOURNE
JOHANNESBURG AUCKLAND

First published 1988
Copyright © Daisy Waugh 1988

British Library Cataloguing in Publication Data

Waugh, Daisy
What is the matter with Mary Jane?
I. Title
823'.914[F]   PR6073.A9/

ISBN 0 434 84390 3

The extract from 'Rice Pudding' by A. A. Milne
is from *When We Were Very Young* and is used by
permission of Methuen Children's Books and the
Canadian publishers, McClelland and Stewart, Toronto.

Printed in Great Britain by
Richard Clay Ltd, Bungay, Suffolk

For Nathaniel, Alexander, Sophia and Julian

What is the matter with Mary Jane?
She's perfectly well and she hasn't a pain,
And it's lovely rice pudding for dinner again, –
What *is* the matter with Mary Jane?

A. A. Milne, 'Rice Pudding'

CHAPTER 1

ISOBEL BURTON'S HUSBAND died of general over-indulgence at
the respectable age of sixty-three. He left behind him a bright
young son of thirteen, Rufus, a nine-week-old baby as yet
unnamed, but later to be called Anna, a beautiful and artistic
bride in her early thirties, an old rectory in Shropshire and a
fairly substantial life-insurance pension.

In 1950 he was forty-nine and his friends (of which there
were few) thought he was not only a confirmed bachelor, but
also vaguely suspected him of being a closet queen. Then he
surprised them all. Just as his contemporaries were reaching
the mid-life crises, he introduced into their élite circle a beautiful and innocent eighteen-year-old girl fresh from school and
new to the city. Very soon afterwards he announced his intention to marry her. He had shown Isobel off, and now he had
no wish to share her. They were to live in the country and
Adam, as he was called, was to retire from the City and live
happily ever after. His friends clicked their tongues in dis-
approval, but they looked at their fat and bitter and middle-
aged wives and secretly they sighed for their lost youth and

their mistresses. They consoled themselves that the marriage wouldn't last. They said that as soon as Isobel grew older and more self-confident she would leave him, and that Adam would crawl back to the City, alone again.

As it happened they did live fairly happily ever afterwards – or rather until he died. Isobel had no close friends, none that she kept up with after her marriage. She had no experience of freedom. She loved her husband and she didn't know what she might be missing.

Adam didn't retire completely when he moved to Shropshire. He knew he would soon be bored with doing nothing all day, and so as a respected member of that county's community he was soon sitting on various important governing boards. He was even a magistrate three days a week in Shrewsbury. Meanwhile, Isobel made a perfect little wife. She was undemanding, amenable, cooked well, she wasn't moody and she had a hobby to keep her occupied during the day. Isobel was creative. She painted pretty water-colours of the local countryside and once a year she exhibited them at a shop in their local town. Her pictures were pleasing and they sold, inexpensively, fairly well. Adam encouraged her. The house was covered with her creations and he proudly pointed them out to passing visitors. He thought it was marvellous that the paintings sold, not that they needed the money. But it gave his wife a feeling of independence that was rather endearing, and it gave her a little extra pocket money. As Isobel grew older she was bored with her water-colours and her artistic style became more adventurous and less accessible. Whether or not they were better paintings, well, I can't comment, they certainly didn't sell so well. But that was long after Adam's death.

Rufus was born exactly nine months after the happy couple's marriage. Adam wanted to hire a nanny, but Isobel refused. She didn't want to stifle her children with too much conventionality, and she remembered the strict small-mindedness of her own nannies. Adam was alarmed by this, but as it had been Isobel's first determined stand since they met, he decided to let it drop. Rufus went to the local village school until he was eight and then he was sent off to prep school, much against Isobel's wishes.

In their thirteenth year of married bliss, Isobel found she was pregnant again. It was a surprise to them both, and although Adam would never have admitted it, he was really quite embarrassed at the prospect of being a father again at the grand age of sixty-two. And Adam certainly didn't look like a young man any more. He was grey, he was fat, he walked with a stoop, he ate too much, he smoked too much and he took no exercise at all. Occasionally Isobel used to worry about him. But it never occurred to her to mention it, and she continued to cook three substantial meals a day.

Anna was born and very soon afterwards Adam died of a heart attack. Isobel sent for Rufus, who was by now in his first year at Rugby. Adam's old accountant dealt with the will and the death duties, and a few weeks after her husband's death he told Isobel that, provided she wasn't too extravagant, she would be able to continue living fairly comfortably at the Rectory and to pay both children's school fees.

The problem was, poor Isobel was rather extravagant. And how could she not be? Her older-man, father-figure husband had never allowed her to worry about finance. He had been rich and he had spoiled her. She didn't understand the meaning of economy. But that wasn't a problem yet. At this point she was a well-heeled and beautiful young widow; give her twenty to thirty years before she runs into trouble.

Rufus never returned to Rugby after his father's death. Isobel's first act of defiance against her late husband had been to send Rufus to a local mixed public day school. He was an out-going boy and he was very happy there, as indeed he had been at Rugby. Years passed and the children grew up and left home. Isobel's painting was by now quite outrageous and

3

incomprehensible. She wore extraordinary clothes, and her faded blonde hair was cropped very close to her head. Gradually all the eligible Shropshire gentlemen began to leave her alone. Her sex life, or the lack of it, was a constant curiosity to those who knew her. Whatever, she was discreet and she never married again.

So at fifty-one she lived alone in her big Rectory. Sometimes she was lonely. She didn't like the county class of person she knew she was supposed to like, the people she had been perfectly content to while away the time with when Adam was alive. But she had her painting, which absorbed her entirely, and she gathered a small group of artistic friends in the neighbourhood.

She seldom thought of the past or of Adam, and when she did it was only with a rather dispassionate fondness. Although she knew she'd been happy in those years, she considered them only as an extended part of her childhood. The new Isobel thought her life (and her art) began after Adam died. Ten years before, when she had read a lot of feminist literature, she used to resent her wasted years and feel quite bitter towards her late husband. But now her political views were more moderate and her memory more blurred.

Rufus and his rather loud but likeable girlfriend used to come and stay quite often – which was more than could be said for Anna who'd only just left home and was still too young to worry about her mother's loneliness. It occurred to Isobel that Rufus might worry too much. He seemed to pity her, but that was probably because he'd never taken her art as more than a hobby. He didn't realise that when she was painting she genuinely wasn't lonely.

Once she went to London and stayed with her son and his girlfriend. But she felt ill at ease and out of place there, and she thought Rufus found it an intrusion upon his privacy, so she didn't go again.

Two years later Isobel was fifty-three, so her children

4

would be thirty-three and twenty respectively. Rufus and Anna were completely unlike, and people still wonder how they were ever sprung from the same loins. But we have seen their mother during that period, and her children's legitimacy couldn't possibly be questioned. It has to be said that they even looked entirely different, but of course there was the age gap, and perhaps after a rest of thirteen years people's genes change, or the creative ability begins to slip. Anna was a mistake. And she was a disaster.

By those in the know, Rufus was considered to be this country's expert on fourteenth-century Italian seascapes. He had written a book on the subject, a long time ago. Now he gave occasional lectures at places like Edinburgh University and once a week he gave a talk about art history in general at Kingston Polytechnic. Rufus led a relatively idle life. He lived with the same loud but likeable girlfriend as he had two years before. She was about his age, perhaps slightly older, and she ran an up-and-coming interior design company in Fulham. She had a private income of her own, which was fortunate since their combined salaries didn't add up to an enormous amount and the two of them liked to live well. They moved with a fairly smart set of arty London people who sometimes offered them coke at the end of dinner parties, and who all talked in that mildly affected languid drawl unique to prom-ising-talent-arty London thirty-year-olds.

Christine and Rufus weren't married, although they had been living together for nearly four years. It wasn't that they disapproved of marriage, just that they were quite happy with life as it was, and they didn't want to threaten their content-ment with any binding promises – or rather Rufus didn't. I'm afraid Christine was beginning to think of settling down and *making babies*, but so far she hadn't voiced her thoughts to her partner (which, you will find, is most unlike Christine).

Despite his red hair and his rather small stocky build, Rufus had always been found attractive, even in adolescence – and fifteen-year-old girls are rarely known to fall for tiny red-heads. In his case they did in their multitudes. He was clever, lazy, witty, badly behaved and charming – perhaps even verging on smooth. That's not to say he wasn't kind, he was kind to a fault. Until Christine came into his life (to the great relief of his poor widowed mother), Rufus had always been attracted to done-down waifs. He had brought home a string of young girls whose fathers were drunks or whose mothers were depressives. One even claimed to have been the victim of an incestuous rape, but she'd had her eye on Rufus for a long time before she found the key to his much-sought-after heart, and it was only then that the shocking story came out.

Anna, on the other hand, was beautiful and clever and hard-working. But she had neither the charm nor the kindness of her elder brother. Never in all her twenty years had she brought a man home (though many had tried their damnedest to get there), nor, come to that, had she ever brought a girl. She found it difficult to make friends, so she had no friends. She hated competing where there was any likelihood of her coming second. So from about ten onwards she gave up any attempt at social small talk, or really any talk at all except 'pass the water' at meal times, and she buried herself in her academic work where, up until Oxbridge, she did brilliantly. When she was twenty she died. Like so many neurotic and competitive teenage girls, she caught the slimming bug, but she was unlucky and she caught it badly. She starved herself to death.

Rufus had been the only person really able to communicate with Anna. With him she would almost relax, she would sneer at her hopeful admirers, occasionally she even used to laugh. She was sharp and her spiteful observations about people and the world made her good company. Rufus used to look forward to the tête-à-têtes with his little sister. In his London life he didn't think of her very often but when he did it was with a vaguely patronising but definite warmth and affection. He was aware of her nervousness and her shyness, and he felt touched that he was the only person able to break through her barriers.

When Christine, who spent a lot of time reading pseudo-psychological books and thought she knew how to work with young people, used to talk rather emphatically to her lover about his little sister's defects and inabilities, Rufus was irritated. Christine always exaggerated in these sessions; she was too melodramatic. She made Anna seem paranoid and jealous, only just on the edge of a breakdown. Rufus never used to listen, and Christine, who was a great one for having people face facts, told him that he was shying away from the truth; that he didn't want to admit everything wasn't right with his life, which was typically male.

In fact Rufus didn't like what Christine told him, and he did see grains of reason in what she said. But he barely admitted it to himself, he certainly wasn't about to admit it to Christine. Poor Christine had a way of putting people's backs up, whether she was talking sense or not. She told Rufus that he, with his superior position in Anna's heart, should try to 'bring her out of herself' a bit, and try to help her build up her self-esteem. It used to annoy Rufus. He thought it was a bit rich, coming from Christine, whom Anna quite clearly couldn't bear, particularly when he was the only person who actually did bring Anna 'out of herself'. If Isobel or Christine ever walked in on one of their happy talks, Anna would shut up, sometimes even in mid-sentence. She would slink to the corner of the room and wait for the first opportunity to get out.

Anna was a secretive girl. She very seldom even confided in Rufus. Once she told him of her ambitions to become an academic, but that was before she failed to get into Oxford. People used to say it broke her heart. Well, it was certainly the beginning of her decline (and indeed the beginning of those heated discussions between Christine and Rufus). This was the first time she hadn't succeeded at something she'd openly tried for. It was a public failure. Another time – it seems like a long time ago now – Anna told Rufus she thought she was too fat and that she was trying to lose a few pounds. Rufus didn't pay much attention at the time, he thought girls always talked about diets. And it was true it wouldn't have hurt her to lose a bit of weight. He can't even remember what he replied to her at the time. But now he rehearses the scene again and again in his mind, he sees it as the first warning light and he missed it. He often wonders if he was to blame for what happened afterwards.

Anna had been nothing but hostile to Christine, as she had been to all the other girls before her. But Christine saw this hostility as jealousy, and doggedly continued trying to befriend her boyfriend's sister. She felt sorry for Anna, which (however irritating Christine may be), is more than most women are prepared to feel for a younger, more beautiful and cleverer girl.

And so it was that on one of Christine's numerous attempts to befriend her future sister-in-law, she and Rufus travelled down to Bristol to visit Anna in her second (miserable) term at the university. Neither of them had seen her since Christmas, when she had already been looking unattractively thin. This was two months later, and although he hated to admit it, Rufus could not deny that Anna was in a very bad way. Christine decided that after leaving Bristol, she should drive straight up to Shropshire to discuss Anna's serious decline with Mrs Burton. Isobel (to us) was alarmed, and she mustn't be blamed for not acting immediately. She hadn't seen Anna for two months, and she was familiar with Christine's exaggeration and love of drama.

Anna rang her mother to say she would be unable to come up to Shropshire during the Easter holidays because she had far too much work to do and she couldn't concentrate with all the distractions at home. Christine, who'd been reading up about anorexia, said this was typical behaviour and that Anna was frightened to return home because she knew her physical changes would cause alarm and that she might be made to eat. Rufus and his mother gritted their teeth and refused to listen.

A month into the summer term, an official from Bristol University telephoned Isobel. He suggested that her daughter take a sabbatical to recuperate.

In despair Isobel rang Christine, who immediately took charge. She saw to it that someone would be there to pick Anna up from Shrewsbury station at the right time, and that her luggage would be sent for afterwards. She also arranged appointments for Anna to see a local psychiatrist.

Well, by now Anna was very ill indeed, and at home she was far from recuperating. Her condition grew worse every day, and three months after her return Anna was too weak to walk unaided. The psychiatrist was of no help. Anna seemed to have given up hope. There was a death-wish about her. Eventually the psychiatrist (and Christine) sent her to a clinic for the mentally ill, where hundreds of analysts tried to help her day and night. But it was too late. Seven weeks later she died. And two months after that, this story begins.

★   ★   ★

It's 1984 and Anna is dead and buried. The family is still waiting for the ground to settle before they put her gravestone up. Isobel who, as I prophesied, is now beginning to feel the pinch and is quite unable to sell any of her masterpieces, still lives alone at the Rectory.

Rufus and Christine took three weeks' compassionate leave from work immediately after Anna died, and the three of them stayed up in Shropshire trying to console one another. It was sad, and it would have been sadder if any of them had noticed it, but none of them actually mourned Anna's removal. They all felt weighed down with an unbearable guilt. They sat endlessly in silence, worrying about each other's suffering. They thought of Anna's wasted life and they thought of the horror of her disease. They thought of the times they had acted too late or too soon, or not at all. They thought, Poor Rufus, Poor Christine, Poor Isobel, but at that stage they didn't miss Anna about the house. She left no spirit there. Her own silent, brooding, miserable presence had been replaced by their own. They thought poor Anna, and they said so. They also thought selfish Anna and they kept it quiet. It only made their guilt heavier and they tried to put it from their minds. During those first weeks of initial shock she was less a person to them than a case of lost opportunity, wasted life, tragedy. Rufus tried hard to remember their happy conversations, but they only reminded him of his own role in Anna's life, and of his blame. You see it mustn't be forgotten, although heaven knows it shouldn't be mentioned, that poor Anna never had been a very nice girl. She'd never been one to spread much sweetness and light.

Christine was wonderful throughout. She rang up the undertakers, organised the funeral, announced Anna's death in *The Times*. It was generally agreed that the funeral would be a quiet one. Anna had made no friends at school or at university, and the family didn't want to see distant cousins and sympathetic neighbours by her grave-side. So it was just the three of them, the coffin-bearers and the priest. A more than usually morbid affair for a beautiful twenty-year-old's final farewell.

For a while after the funeral, Isobel could at least occupy herself by answering the condolence letters. But there weren't an enormous number and it was hardly a thankful task, particularly as she had so little to say about her only daughter. She had really known very little about her, and I'm afraid to say she hadn't taken as much trouble as she could have done to find out. She was aware of that.

Christine, with her great psychological insight and a slightly more objective attitude towards Anna's death – she only really suffered for Rufus – had a much more complex reason for her guilt. Firstly, she decided she hadn't bullied Isobel or Rufus to take positive action nearly soon enough. She should have forced Anna to see a psychiatrist when she first noticed her decline at Bristol. But that was unrealistic. She couldn't force Anna or Rufus or Isobel to do anything they didn't want to do. But for some sort of masochistic reason, she refused to accept that. Secondly, Christine had always been aware of Anna's overwhelming jealousy of the place Christine held in Rufus's heart. Anna starved herself in an attempt to attract his attention, but she failed because Christine had been in the way.

Three weeks after Anna's death Isobel was once again left alone in Shropshire. Rufus asked her if she wanted to stay with them in London, but she refused. She said she had neglected her painting for far too long, and that it was time she carried on with her life. Rufus was rather puzzled by the last bit, but he smiled sympathetically and left her behind.

Of course poor Isobel didn't get it together to pick up her paintbrush for a while. She spent her days moving listlessly from room to empty room, remembering all the times she'd shown what could have been interpreted as favouritism to her son or unfairness to Anna during their childhood. She remembered the time she hadn't been bothered to congratulate Anna enthusiastically enough for her fifty-fifth excellent school report (the same day Isobel had managed to sell one of her new-style paintings, which was a much rarer occurrence). Anna had lost her temper and sulked, unnoticed because it was so like her usual behaviour, for two weeks into the summer holidays.

Sometimes Isobel stood on the threshold of her daughter's old bedroom. When Anna was moved to the clinic (with just three nightdresses and a toothbrush), Christine tactlessly suggested that the two of them clear out Anna's bedroom. Everyone knew that she was about to die. Isobel, understandably, had been sickened by the idea and steadfastly refused to do any such thing. Christine didn't suggest it again after her death. And the room still had a pair of scrumpled, child-size jeans lying on the floor. Her diary was half sticking out from under the bed. Isobel knew it had to be cleared, and every time she thought she was feeling strong she tried to start. But the jeans made her feel ill. They were too small and too alive.

Otherwise she read endless letters from her accountant warning her to stop spending money, because she was seriously in debt, and she bought a video recorder and a lot of Danielle Steeles to take her mind off things, which of course they didn't. She sat through *ET* and *Arthur* and *The Pink Panther Strikes Again*. She had been told they were funny and that they would cheer her up. That was nonsense. She just watched the moving screen, or stared at the same page of her romantic rotter, and thought about Anna.

She stared at a picture where Anna was caught smiling, and gradually in her lonely hours, Isobel began to create a fictional character behind the smile. She even invented silly little things, like 'Anna used to love wearing green', 'Anna had the most extraordinary passion for Tintin'.

To give Isobel her due, her creation was not absolute invention. She had only a blurred memory of her daughter before her *malaise*. And she wanted to remember Anna in the healthy days, when she was even quite well rounded. She had a clear picture of Anna on Christmas night about four years ago. She wore a very pretty straight green dress that clung, perhaps slightly too much, around her bottom. In Isobel's mind, Anna was smiling. She remembered the evening was a happy one.

Isobel drew strength from her hazily remembered, heavily elaborated family scenes. She and Anna playing tennis. Anna winning, Anna happy, Isobel telling a thirteen-year-old Anna about the facts of life, Anna looking bored, but at ease with her mother's confidences (which is highly unlikely). Anna advising Isobel on her wardrobe, their going on wildly extravagant shopping sprees together in South Molton Street. Anna passing her driving test. Isobel buying her a car.

As the months passed by, Isobel almost believed she could forget the time when Anna used to lie silently, day after day, in Isobel's studio as she painted, just waiting to die. She had tried hard during that time to improve relations with Anna, but she had little understanding of her daughter, and even less of her daughter's disease. The recuperation attempt was a disaster, and Isobel – as well she might – blamed herself for it somewhat.

Meanwhile, back in London, Christine and Rufus had an unspoken policy never to mention his sister's name. They filled their time going to trendy drinking houses in Notting Hill Gate and expensive restaurants in Soho, and they saw even more friends than they usually did. Their friends had the same unspoken policy. They'd only heard about Anna's death in rumour and they vaguely preferred to pretend that they knew nothing about it. I suppose they were embarrassed. Anyway, Rufus liked it that way.

Christine still read a lot of psychological books with chapters on anorexia and by now she really was quite an expert. She silently agreed not to talk of Anna, but she still thought it was her duty to make sure Rufus came to terms with his sister's death. She found a wonderful method to deal with it. And poor Rufus was too weak or too lazy to ask her to stop. Even at breakfast (at which she insisted he was present even though he had no job of work to go to most days – she'd learnt togetherness at breakfast was very important for an enduring relationship), she told him unnecessary facts about his later sister's complaint.

'Did you know anorexics shave off their pubic hair?'
'No.'

'It's a significant symptom; you see they're trying to revert back to childhood, they can't cope with adult life. And actually it's an interesting irony that at about the same stage of the illness, the hair on their heads begins to fall out anyway because of malnutrition.'

'Mmm.'

'It's no good just sounding bored and hoping I'll shut up. You ought to know these things, Rufus, you can't just block yourself off from other people's suffering. People *do* get this disease, and its spreading. Over one and a half million girls (and boys) at this moment in Britain have got what's termed as an "unhealthy attitude towards their eating patterns". You should be able to recognise an early victim, or even a potential victim, and prevent all that suffering before the illness actually takes root in the young person's mind. Although, of course, as I'm sure you know, it isn't just restricted to middle-class adolescent girls, well, I suppose they do make up the majority of cases, but post-natal women and even women during their menopause have been known to fall prey . . .'

And all this at an enforced early morning breakfast. It *can't* have helped towards their enduring relationship. Poor Rufus.

As soon as Christine left for work these days, Rufus, rather uncharacteristically, had taken to going for a run. When he came back he lit a cigarette, which is more than most of us can manage, and then, if he could summon up the energy, he might do some research on the biography that he'd been working on for two and a half years. But that didn't happen very often, so by ten o'clock he had the rest of the day to fill and nothing to do until Christine came home. It was a shame she wouldn't leave him to sleep, because recently between ten and seven when Christine came home Rufus had taken to spending the days drinking and sitting at his empty desk crying for his mother and Anna and for all the disgusting facts that his girlfriend might have told him that morning about his little sister's disease.

Rufus wasn't a tremendously reflective man. He acted almost entirely on his emotions and his laziness. He thought that apart from the obvious great sadness of Anna, he liked his lifestyle. But how could he possibly when he really had nothing to do? And when the one thing that he was supposed to specialise in couldn't hold his attention more often than once a fortnight, when he used to work half-heartedly for a morning researching his book? He thought he loved his girlfriend. Well, he may have been fond of her and comfortable with her, but can he really love a girl who, however kind she is trying to be, is capable of being so sickeningly tactless at breakfast time?

One morning in February, as he sat in his unused study, just after his daily run, he decided he shouldn't just cry for his mother, he should go down and stay with her. He hadn't been down for nearly two months (not since the three weeks' compassionate leave), and he had barely even talked to her. Although dutiful Christine had telephoned her almost every day. Christine said there were problems about money at home, on top of everything else. So Rufus rose from his tear-stained desk, packed his bag, left a note on the kitchen table for his lover and caught the next train to Shrewsbury.

He took a taxi for the six-mile journey from the station to home; he rather childishly wanted to surprise his mother and see her face light up with surprise when he walked into her studio. Rufus didn't know his mother hadn't been painting for the last three months, and I'm afraid to say that apart from the fact that it reflected her bad state of mind, Rufus wouldn't have minded too much. He'd often tried to appreciate his mothers artistry, but try as he might he couldn't really find much pleasure in her enormous, frenzied, dull-coloured canvases. Rufus remembered how shockingly spiteful and funny Anna had been in private about their mother's talent.

Poor Rufus's eventual arrival at the Rectory wasn't so gallant or moving as he had planned it to be. He discovered he didn't have enough change to tip the cab driver. And his mother found him scrabbling around in the bowl on the hall table looking for any loose change he could find, with the driver impatiently revving his engine in the background.

Apparently the cleaning lady had been ill for the last three days and the house was already in a mess. Rufus noticed immediately and he wasn't particularly observant. He also noticed that the house didn't smell like it usually did. It took him a while to realise it was the absence of white spirit and oil paint in the air that made the Rectory seem so unfamiliar. So Isobel hadn't been painting. It worried him.

He was still more worried when the next morning (and the fourth day that the cleaning lady hadn't come in) he saw the very same cleaning lady greet him warmly and robustly in the village shop. He told her that she seemed much better and that they were missing her up at the Rectory. Mrs Grenville (as she was called), looked first puzzled and then embarrassed. She said Mrs Burton had asked her to come in only once a fortnight from now on, what with the house being so empty . . . and the prices being what they were. Mrs Grenville looked sly, as if she were letting drop an incredibly important clue, which indeed she was.

So Isobel could no longer afford a cleaning lady; oh dear, oh dear. He strode back to the house thinking it was high time the two of them had a man to man talk about finance. Isobel was so evasive as soon as the subject of money came up. She couldn't bear thinking about it, probably because by now her debts were pretty big.

Anna's bill at the clinic hadn't been paid off yet, and that, Rufus knew for some reason (probably through Christine who was fascinated by all aspects of private medicine), had cost £125 a day.

But Rufus couldn't talk about money when he got home, because a very earnest local potter who'd just started an Open University degree was calling on his mother armed with a lot of vegetarian pasties for a surprise luncheon. The lady had heard of Rufus on a professional basis and wanted to discuss Art, so poor Rufus was forced to talk for two hours with her in a very slow, polite voice about Interesting Artists He Had Known, while his mother, who clearly didn't like her one bit (that at least was a relief), wandered off round the house mumbling about open windows and banging doors. The unwelcome caller eventually finished her horrible pastie and left. She gushed her appreciation at being able to meet such a distinguished man, and in spite of himself, Rufus felt a certain swelling in the bosom. Maybe the pasties weren't so bad after all. He said goodbye warmly and begged her to come calling again.

By the time the woman left, so had Rufus's great resolution. He knew Isobel found money an unpleasant topic, and she was having a hard enough time as it was. He would wait until she was feeling stronger.

At tea-time the two of them played backgammon in the drawing room. Rufus asked his mother how her painting was going in an overly offhand voice.

'Oh, not too bad, but I can't seem to find anything to represent these days; perhaps I've over-stretched myself as an artist. That woman who came to lunch showed a great interest in one I showed her before you arrived. She said she'd get in touch. It sounds like she'll buy it, and I'm charging quite a hefty sum.'

The woman had been fairly rude to Rufus, by inference, about Isobel's art. But he chose not to comment. Both he and his mother were great optimists, only his optimism was kept in order by Christine and by a small amount of realism. There was no point in shattering Isobel's illusions now, not after all she'd been through.

Or at least that's what Rufus thought. I'm not sure if he was entirely right. Isobel had to stop spending money and her art was bringing in nothing.

Neither of them were really concentrating on their game, but they followed it through to the end half-heartedly. Isobel won and then the telephone rang. Rufus answered and a man called Andrew with a young, smooth voice asked if he could speak to his mother. Isobel took the call in the library and came back some time later looking quite refreshed. Rufus wondered again about his mother's sex life. He didn't really like to dwell on Andrew's relationship with his mother – but she was old and lonely and he *supposed* it didn't matter, if indeed there was even a case. As long as Christine didn't get hold of any ideas, or Heaven only knew what would make up their conversations at breakfast.

For a while they didn't say anything. Then Rufus began to feel a bit uncomfortable, so he decided to go to the lavatory. When he came back Isobel told him that Christine had rung and she had bought a dog. The two of them were driving up from London tomorrow evening after work.

Rufus thought, Then tomorrow must be Friday.

On the whole he was pleased with the news. He wondered what kind of dog it was, and who would look after it when they went abroad. He decided that would be his mother's job. It would take her mind off things for a while at least.

So the next day was a Friday, and as was planned, Christine and the dog travelled up together from London. She disliked the idea of Isobel and Rufus being alone together. She thought it was *all too morbid*, and anyway they probably wouldn't be able to get themselves any proper meals. Although she did think it was high time Isobel learnt to fend for herself a bit. But she supposed that as long as she and Rufus were there to look after her, she'd never learn.

Sometimes Christine thought she resented the way the Burton family relied on her so heavily. Actually, she quite liked the idea of resenting it.

She arrived at nine, and although she'd told them not to wait, she rather assumed that they would. She'd even brought down some fresh pasta from the local Italian shop for supper, and she was looking forward to it. Christine felt smug when she thought of their delight when they compared her bounty with the usual packeted ham and baked potatoes they would be planning to sit down to.

She was furious when she saw the big, square, healthy meal they had just begun when she arrived. She *thought* she thought they could have waited, but for all her psychological insight and woman's intuition, we know better. Christine was slightly comforted when they told her the supper was the work of the cleaning lady (before she retired) and that they had only got it out of the deep-freeze.

Christine feigned her good humour throughout dinner, and the three of them passed the evening discussing the antics of Christine's (admittedly divine) new Labrador puppy. It was a female and Christine was determined that it should be called Anastasia – but it would inevitably become Anna for short. Oh dear. So she changed it to Fortunata.

After dinner Isobel said she would leave the young people alone, and she went to bed. At last Rufus could pour out the troubles with the cleaning lady. At last Christine cheered up. She *was* needed after all. Rufus had sensed Christine's indignation about supper, and he decided it would be wise to make excuses for it before he worried her with Isobel's finances. Christine said she didn't know what he was talking about. She had told them not to wait and it was a great relief to see them feeding themselves properly, although she had to admit it was a surprise. And anyway, the pasta could wait for tomorrow's lunch – unless, of course, he had any other surprise feasts ready and waiting for them in the deep-freeze. Rufus laughed at that, not because he thought he was meant to, or because he found it particularly funny. He laughed because he thought it was probably the best way out of a difficult situation and he wanted to move on to the next topic.

Christine was worried when she heard what Rufus had to

tell her. The two of them spent several hours trying to calculate exactly how much Isobel was in debt, what her overall annual expenditure and income was, or whether her income hadn't actually dried up entirely. They thought of pieces of furniture that could be sold. And then they could always sell Anna's car, which at this moment was just rotting down beside the tennis court. It was only three and a half years old.

By four o'clock that morning, they had moved from the drawing room back into the kitchen; they were feeling slightly sick with all the cups of coffee swilling around in their insides, and they had run out of cigarettes. They'd found no proper solution, really, because they didn't have the facts, and they were even quite bored with the whole topic. Christine got up and said it was time for bed. Then she said what Rufus had half been hoping, half dreading, she would say all evening:

'I'll speak to your mother about it first thing in the morning.'

And she did.

CHAPTER 2

CHRISTINE DIDN'T GET very far with her talk the next morning. She took Isobel into Isobel's library and said it was time they discussed money. Just as she was deceiving herself that the two of them were getting to the heart of the matter they were interrupted by the telephone. Isobel leapt to answer it, thanking God for the diversion. It was her accountant. Christine recognised the name. And she noticed a humility in Isobel's voice that had been absolutely absent a minute before. Christine sat tight. She listened hard and gathered that he wanted to meet Isobel urgently. Isobel said she didn't know, she was very busy, there was a new dog in the house, and a potter in the neighbourhood had shown a great interest in one of her paintings. It sounded desperate and suddenly Christine felt overcome with pity for this new-born, aggressively independent, totally incompetent old woman.

Isobel hung up. There was an embarrassed silence; evidently the accountant hadn't been too impressed by Isobel's hopeful news. The two of them were to meet for lunch on Monday. Christine opened her mouth. She spoke more gently this time.

'Have you ever thought of selling anything? Rufus and I were discussing it last night – you must have some pretty valuable stuff here, and there's Anna's car that's just rotting outside. We could sell that tomorrow.'

Isobel was trying to think of a tart reply to end the conversation and to put Christine back in her place when she heard her son shouting about the dog in the hall. Her face relaxed, saved by the bell again.

The door opened. 'Where's that fucking dog? It's just shat all over our bedroom floor. Oh, hello mother, I thought you were in your studio.'

Rufus had entirely forgotten the plans he and Christine made the night before. He was rather surprised to see the rapture with which his mother greeted his news. Christine pulled a meaningful face at him and said nothing. Rufus looked absolutely blank and asked her what was the matter. Isobel leapt to her feet and said she thought she'd seen the dog in the garden. She almost ran out of the room. Rufus shouted in vain after her not to worry, he could look out for it himself. Then he shrugged his shoulders, not terribly worried, and asked Christine what on earth was the matter with the two of them.

Christine was extremely annoyed. She thought she'd just been handling a very delicate subject rather well.

'Is your memory really as short as it seems to be, or are you just pretending because in some idiotic twisted way you think it's attractive? For Christ's sake Rufus, it's *your* bloody mother, not mine.'

Rufus realised he'd interrupted something important. But then everything was important to Christine. After a moment's bewilderment at her outburst, he remembered what it was all about. Then he felt genuinely sorry.

Christine's temper was soothed fairly soon, and whose wouldn't be when Rufus looked so hang-dog, and apologised so whole-heartedly? He had always been one of the boys who got away with giving in essays late at school. (The jealous ones used to say in grown-up voices that his results would suffer for it. It was annoying because his results did, and the prefects were proved right, which was very bad for their characters.)

Anyway, once Christine was calmer and Isobel was still supposedly looking for the dog, Rufus asked about what had been said. Christine waffled for a while; she had very little to report. She said it would help if they had some figures, and that she would find the accountant's telephone number and ring him from work on Monday. Rufus thought that was probably a very good idea, but that they must make sure the accountant didn't tell Isobel anything about it.

The next problem was the art, or rather the lack of it, or rather Isobel's slightly shaky state of mind. None of them mentioned Anna's name over the weekend and Christine even left her anorexic books and facts in London. Rufus thought it was unfair the way he had to hear about pubic hairs when his mother didn't. And he found it odd that Christine seemed to think Isobel had no need for her guidance in dealing with Anna's death. Well, he was wrong there. She had a plan she'd thought out only this morning. It still wasn't absolutely formed, but when it was she thought it would solve all Isobel's problems in one go. She would tell Rufus the first half of it when they got back to London.

So it surprised Rufus when Christine said, just before the door opened to let in Isobel and the dog, that they would let everything drop until Monday, and just relax and enjoy themselves. Rufus trusted Christine, and he was pleased to agree with the plan.

Isobel came in talking slightly too enthusiastically about where she'd found the dog and how they'd never guess what it had been doing. They all laughed when she told them and agreed that that was very sweet and proved how clever the dog was sure to be.

Rufus said what about a drink and let's have lunch. Then Isobel suddenly threw her hand to her mouth and screamed. She'd forgotten she'd asked the Woodrows for lunch and it was already half-past twelve – they would arrive any minute. Christine's pasta was bought for three, and it couldn't possibly be divided between seven. The Woodrows' daughter and her husband were down for the weekend, too.

Rufus was quite pleased when he heard that. In their county days, when he'd been about fifteen, the Woodrow daughter and he had hung around quite a lot together at various parties. They used to complain about the awfulness of the other people in the room. He supposed she had been his first proper walk-out really, and he hadn't seen her since she was married, which must be nearly ten years ago now.

Christine strode towards the kitchen telling Isobel not to worry. She would be able to rustle something up. (And even Christine doubted the truth of her words this time; the larder was empty, everything was in the deep-freeze except the pasta.)

Rufus knew his mother hadn't mixed with the local gentry for years now; he asked her why on earth she had invited them to lunch. Isobel was strangely put out by the question. She said rather defensively that the Woodrows had been very good friends when she first moved to Shropshire and knew no one. She said that just because Rufus may be fickle enough to desert people once they'd served their purpose, even if they were lonely and sad, then she supposed that that was his business. But he wasn't to expect his mother to be so heartless.

Rufus apologised and thought he was really being given a tough time this morning. He asked, just by way of keeping the conversation rolling, how long ago Isobel had invited them.

It seemed to Rufus that his mother wasn't herself at all today. She answered that she wouldn't have dreamt of inviting them if she'd known her son was down for the weekend. She

24

knew how snobbish he was about his childhood friends and neighbours. She was sorry for him that the company his mother kept in the country was so dim compared to what he was used to in London, and eventually she said that she'd invited them about a fortnight ago.

At last Rufus understood why his mother was being so defensive. She had been lonely and depressed. She couldn't face ringing her arty friends because they would ask how her painting was coming along and she would have to admit that it wasn't going along at all. She'd wanted to see people and to see people who wouldn't be a threat. So she rang what must have been the oldest and dimmest friends she could muster. The Woodrows were kind and they were loyal. Unlike the rest of the county set, they had continued to keep in touch with Isobel. But Isobel had systematically refused to have anything to do with them for fifteen years.

When Rufus worked all that out, he felt a lump rise in his throat. You see, Rufus is a compassionate man, but he's also a bit of a cry-baby. He turned his face towards the drinks' tray and poured himself some gin and tonic. By then he was sufficiently recovered to ask his mother what she would like to drink.

Isobel didn't generally bear grudges. But suddenly she thought of her conversation with Christine, and then of the one she'd just had with her son, and she felt a great wave of resentment – anger – rise up inside her. I suppose she felt her pride was being threatened. And she was right. It had not been a serene or dignified Sunday morning for her. So she said in a tight voice that she wouldn't have a drink just yet, thank you. Then she picked up a magazine and pretended to read it until she thought she'd calmed down.

Christine came out of the kitchen saying it was hopeless. They couldn't possibly feed seven people on the food in the house. But not to worry, she still had one more idea. It was at times like this that Rufus realised how much he loved

Christine. She would go down to the local pub and try to buy some kind of food from the landlord. This was generally agreed to be a good idea. Rufus said he was pretty chummy with the publican and that perhaps he ought to go. Anyway, he needed to buy some cigarettes.

Isobel told her son not to use the word chummy because it was coy and embarrassing. Rufus beamed. It was the first time since Anna's illness that she sounded like her old self. He laughed and said she was too sensitive about the language and why didn't she give up painting and write a novel. Isobel shuddered with embarrassment again, and immediately leapt to the defence of her art. Christine just watched. She didn't really understand what was wrong with the word chummy anyway. But she was glad to see Rufus's grin. She remembered how attractive it was and realised it had been missing for a long time.

Rufus was collecting his money and Isobel was left alone with Christine. Christine poured herself a drink and sat down. But Isobel suddenly became restless. She said the dog must need taking for a walk, so she decided to accompany Rufus to the pub and take the dog. Even Christine couldn't say, 'It's all right, I've got a secret plan, and I'm not going to bully you about money for the time being.' So she took her drink into the kitchen and started to lay the table.

The Woodrows arrived before the other two came back from the pub. Christine decided that when in difficulty one should always tell the truth. She told the Woodrows that Isobel had entirely forgotten about their arrival until half an hour ago. And that she and Rufus had just popped down to the pub to see if they could cadge some scraps off the publican. Then she laughed and introduced herself as Rufus's long-standing girlfriend.

The Woodrows stood in an embarrassed huddle by the drawing-room door and waited to be offered a drink. They made some boring comments about the weather and then said it was odd how bad the hunting season had been that year. Christine stopped pouring Mrs Woodrow's Punt-e-mes and looked up. Then she smiled and said, 'Oh dear, I'm afraid I don't hunt.'

The daughter tried to ease the atmosphere by giggling and saying, 'Mummy's absolutely hopeless. She can't believe that everyone isn't as fascinated with country sports as she is.'

Christine laughed and told them all to sit down.

'Have you known Isobel long?'

Mr Woodrow laughed and said, 'Oh good heavens, we've known Isobel since before you were born I should think.'

For some reason that annoyed Christine, so she turned to the daughter's husband and asked what he did. He looked like a very dull, Sloaney man, and Christine assumed he either worked in the City or as an estate agent.

The Woodrow daughter answered for her husband, 'Albert works at Sturgis. So he has great fun every day showing beautiful young girls around beautiful old properties, don't you, darling?'

'Well, I wouldn't say so exactly. Actually, most of our clients are men. But you do get the occasional little knockout trying her hand in the property game.' He laughed, but Christine didn't.

She said, 'If you don't mind me saying so, Albert, I take exception to that remark. What, exactly, do you mean by a *little knockout?*'

Mr and Mrs Woodrow were talking amongst themselves. They were discussing, with a great deal more volume than was necessary, Isobel's art. They still had a few of her very early pictures hanging in one of the spare bedrooms.

Albert laughed uneasily and said, 'Oh Gawd, we've got a feminist in our midst.'

Christine pounced. 'You see, that's a clear example of the stupid, defensive, facetious barrier that men put up between

27

themselves and the women's movement. And it has to be broken down.'

The daughter looked stunned, but she tended to agree with Christine. After a while she said, 'Honestly, Albert, sometimes I think your attitudes went out with the Ark.' Then she giggled again, and the giggle was beginning to get on Christine's nerves.

By now Albert was feeling quite out of his depth. He shifted his rather large bulk to the other side of the chair and he was blushing.

'No, but to be serious for a minute,' he said, 'I do see your point of view; however the fact remains . . .'

Christine was enjoying herself; she was a natural bully. But they were interrupted. Just then Isobel, the dog and Rufus charged through the door apologising. They hadn't realised what time it was. They'd just been taking the dog for a walk. Isobel looked desperate. Obviously the outing had been a failure.

Rufus said, 'Sindy,' in an affected warm voice, and walked across the room towards her with his arms stretched out and his head on one side. Rufus still rather fancied the Sloaney daughter who was smiling warmly up at him from the sofa. He wanted to be alluring and he thought he was smiling with his eyes. They kissed each other and went off into a corner of the room to flirt and talk about old times. Christine overheard some of their conversation and noticed that 'Sindy' was slightly more sparky with Rufus than she had been with her husband. Christine glowered at the estate agent, who didn't pay any attention because he was complimenting Isobel on her garden.

Neither party was mentioning lunch, and it was half-past one. Christine tried to draw Rufus aside to question him about it. But he wouldn't come away, so eventually she just walked right up to the childhood sweethearts and asked her boyfriend what was happening about lunch. Rufus looked at Christine for a moment in horror, and before the daughter could make any comment to ease the situation, he said:

'Darling, had you forgotten? We're having a late lunch with the Connors. Don't you remember Mummy rang them up yesterday to warn them we'd be a bit late because our old friends the Woodrows were coming for a drink before lunch?'

Rufus laughed smoothly; he was pleased with the way he'd delivered his lines (he and Isobel had put them together just outside the drawing-room door). Then he added to Sindy. 'You'd think she was going senile and she's only thirty-three.'

Christine stared at her lover in amazement. Then she looked at Sindy who was doing the same thing. For once she was lost for words, so she said, 'Oh,' and wandered away looking dazed.

Well, the Woodrows stayed and stayed. They didn't dare to mention lunch and they didn't dare to leave. At about three o'clock Sindy took her parents aside and mumbled something in their ears. The parents looked as though they understood, because they began to collect their effects and make noises about leaving. Albert said:

'But I thought we were invited here for . . .' and the whole room burst into loud conversation, mostly about Christine's enchanting new puppy. The Woodrows left smiling very hard and promising to get in touch in the spring. Only Albert looked rather cross and bewildered.

Christine went straight into the kitchen to cook the pasta. Rufus and Isobel followed her and she told them how she'd explained their absence to the Woodrows before they arrived. At first they were horrified, but as the strain of the afternoon began to lessen and they ate their long-awaited pasta, they laughed. They laughed quite hard, and it was a refreshing sound in that empty house of unmentioned mourning.

Christine and Rufus left the Rectory before supper and drove back to London. After a great deal of discussion it was generally decided that the dog would be much happier left up in Shropshire. And as Isobel had genuinely grown so fond of it, she agreed to keep it. She pretended that she was doing the young couple a favour but no one was deceived, least of all herself. Christine pretended to be disappointed to see the dog go, but she was pleased to see just the first step in her Grand Plan already taking shape so easily.

They didn't talk much on the way home. Rufus asked Christine if she'd always intended to leave the dog with Isobel. Christine was pleased by the question, and she pulled a mysterious face, 'Perhaps I did, perhaps I didn't.'

'Sindy's changed a lot, she's grown rather dull in her old age. When she was young she was by far the best of the bunch. Wasn't her husband ghastly?'

'God, I hated him; you should have heard what he said about "little knockouts" before you arrived. Actually, you arrived just in time to prevent what promised to be quite an exciting argument. I think his wife is a bit crushed by him, she at least had a bit more spunk than he did. But she kept giggling. No, actually she was pretty dull, too. What on earth made your mother want to invite them?'

Christine hadn't been expecting an answer to the question, and she was rather irritated by the full and passionate answer that she got. First of all she saw that Rufus was right, which I'm afraid was irritating enough in itself, next she wished she'd been the one to notice it and the one in a position to explain it patiently to Isobel's son, and finally she thought that psychological insight was her province and that Rufus was poaching. After all, she was only too ready to ask for his opinion about art.

So after Rufus explained and Christine said, 'Oh, of course I'd noticed that already', which didn't really make much sense, they drove in silence.

By eleven o'clock the two of them were back in their flat in Paddington eating a fairly nasty Chinese take-away. Rufus asked Christine whether she'd worked out a way to solve his mother's problems. She said she had, but that she had to ring Isobel's accountant to see if it was possible.

'You may not like the idea,' she warned. She knew he wouldn't like the idea.

'I love all your ideas,' he said.

Christine looked pleased – and smug. 'Not this one you won't.'

They finished the Chinese take-away – actually it really was quite disgusting and they threw most of it away. Then they went to bed.

★   ★   ★

Christine came back from work the next evening victorious. She had talked to the accountant, who couldn't have been more co-operative, and everything was possible. Rufus looked as pleased as he could muster, but he was feeling a bit hung over and a bit liverish. He'd only just returned from a very heavy lunch with an old friend. Christine made him a cup of coffee, sat him down and tried to think of the best way to explain her plan. Suddenly she felt rather nervous. She knew how much Rufus valued the relative solidity of his old home. It provided a comfortable contrast to the deaths and drunken lunches and empty days that otherwise made up his lifestyle.

She began, 'Obviously it would be out of the question to sell the Rectory, although of course we both know that it's by far your mother's most valuable asset.'

'Exactly,' said Rufus.

Christine looked slightly taken aback. She glanced up at him. Then she looked back at her right hand which was gently hitting the table to stress, say, every third word or so.

'Right. So we've got a house that nobody wants to sell. It's a pretty big house. It's far too big for the one person who lives in it, and who can't even afford to have it cleaned. OK?'

'Just what are you getting at, Chris?' Rufus interrupted, and Christine ignored him.

'We've got a lonely woman, your mother, who can't sell her paintings – and can't even paint at the moment anyway. Right. So she's got time on her hands and she's broke. What does she do all day? Well, you tell me. I have a suspicion she does sweet fanny all. So she just sits and mopes about your little sister.'

Rufus winced and Christine either chose not to, or actually didn't, notice. She continued.

'Put all that together, and what have we got?'

'She needs help.'

'Exactly, as you say, someone who is badly in need of help. So what should we do?'

Rufus began to feel a bit annoyed. Who did she think she was, Hercule Poirot? Still he wanted to know what she intended to do, So he played along.

'That's just what I don't know. What *can* we do?'

Suddenly Christine changed tack. She stopped beating her hand against the table, and she said in a quieter voice, looking into Rufus's eyes all the while, 'What would you think of sharing your house, Rufus?'

'What?'

'Look, there are a lot of rooms just being wasted up there. We could change the place into a rest home for retired gentle folks.'

Rufus looked horrified.

'Or how about just a bed and breakfast? It's a pretty house, so there wouldn't be a shortage of willing paying guests. All we need is a grant from the council to help us renovate it and to instal new bathrooms, knock down walls and all that. It would give your mother something to think about. She'd be meeting new people every day – and you know, I think when we're not there she can sometimes go for a fortnight without seeing a soul, except the village shopkeeper. The Woodrows were clearly a one-off, and anyway, they're hardly what you'd call company. You know, I fear for her sanity.'

That sentence stirred unpleasant memories in Rufus's mind. Christine had said that about Anna, and he had refused to listen. In fact it was that sentence that decided him. He wasn't going to make the same mistake twice. This time he would listen to Christine before it was too late. How could he be so selfish as to dream of keeping the house as it was just for his own peace of mind and the occasional weekend at the cost of his mother's sanity? The bed and breakfast (an up-market one, mind), was a good idea. It would make money, and it would keep his mother occupied.

Perfect. Christine had won the first round much more easily than she thought she would. It didn't occur to her that it was only just one sentence that had in fact forced poor Rufus's guilty hand.

But still the big battle was ahead. Isobel had yet to be persuaded, and Christine didn't have an idea how she was going to tackle that one. She thought back to her brief money conversation with Isobel at the weekend. She was forced to admit that, honestly, she hadn't done too brilliantly. Of course, there had been interruptions, and maybe she really had been getting to the bottom of it when bloody Rufus burst in looking for the dog. Christine, who was no coward, didn't really relish the idea of discussing beds and breakfasts with proud, unreasonable Isobel. Perhaps Rufus should be allowed to handle this one. She'd think about it.

CHAPTER 3

BUT RUFUS WHO was sitting in his empty study once more, had been thinking about the problem too. He didn't want to push his luck and he knew Christine and her ideas were a godsend to the family. But he was fairly sure that the task of suggesting such a monumental change in her life to Isobel should definitely fall on his shoulders. Christine was a wonderful woman, and Rufus knew that she had great depths of understanding, but it would be difficult for her to understand how a woman such as Isobel, who was quite so down on her luck, would be bound to cling hard to her last bastion of security and respectability. Rufus knew there wasn't much respectable about a bed and breakfast. And Isobel, for all her modern ideas and Bohemian friends, was still quite a snob underneath. She wouldn't like her living standards to drop quite so drastically or so visibly. No, she would not be proud of her B & B.

So when Christine returned from work the next day, both she and Rufus had the same unspoken suggestion to put to the other. The problem was to negotiate it without wounding Christine's pride. And she handled it beautifully.

Christine poured herself a drink and began.

'Darling, I've been thinking about this plan for the Rectory . . .'

'So have I.'

She looked up, alarmed. 'You haven't changed your mind, have you?'

'No, no, no, no, no, it's just that . . .'

Christine interrupted. 'That's all right then. Keep quiet for a minute, will you? Just let me finish first. I think this is important.

'Has it ever occurred to you that your mother may think I do too much for you?'

'What?'

'Well, I just thought that actually your mother may be rather hurt. You see it's always me who rings her up in the country, it was me who drew her aside about the money last weekend and I won't mention Anna, but I played a very supportive role in all that too. I'm not complaining, I mean, *I* know how much you care about your mother but does she? I wonder if she thinks you don't really worry about her as much as you should. For all she knows, you may just think of her as a tiresome burden. I'm not saying she's self-pitying or anything, but you are the only member of her family left alive . . . Do you see what I'm getting at?'

Rufus was horrified. This was far more important than what he had been interrupted from saying. And no, it never *had* occurred to him. God, he was so selfish, why couldn't he look outwards a bit more, like Christine was always telling him to, then he might notice these things before it was too late. Of course he loved his mother.

'So what can I do?'

'I think it would probably be a good idea if I took a step back for once, and let you take over discussions with your mother about the bed and breakfast. I know it's a very difficult thing to ask you to do, but it may just be your chance to redeem yourself – if you need to, which of course I'm not stating categorically that you do. I'm sure I don't need to remind you, she's a desperate, broken, lonely woman.'

If Rufus hadn't been in such a state of self-hatred, he would have objected to Christine's brutal, melodramatic description of his mother, but he was so relieved that his brilliant Christine had not only identified a big problem, but also come out with an immediate answer to it, that he just gasped with relief and threw his arms around her.

Christine disentangled herself a little irritably. 'So what do you think?'

'I think you're the most brilliant, sensitive, thoughtful, lovely person I've ever had the fortune to meet up with. And I think you're absolutely right. God, why the hell didn't I notice it before?'

Rufus had entirely forgotten that that was exactly what he intended to suggest to Christine when the conversation began.

Christine got up. 'Right, so that's settled then. Now we just have to think about the details. We've got to work out your angle.'

Rufus watched her adoringly, and it was on the tip of his tongue to ask Christine to marry him there and then. But he stopped himself. He thought Christine would say he was being middle-aged and bourgeois. If he only knew.

The two of them were going out to dinner with some people that they didn't know very well or like very much. But that wasn't particularly extraordinary. Christine said they would have to discuss the details at breakfast. They didn't have time now. She went away to run a bath and think about what she was going to wear. Rufus poured himself another drink and lit a cigarette. He wasn't going to change this evening.

The man whose dinner party it was worked at the BBC, and his girlfriend worked on magazines. Rufus groaned to himself; he hated magazine girls.

Half an hour later, Christine came back into the drawing room, all spruced up. The room was filled with her scent and Rufus felt slightly sick. He stubbed out his cigarette in the overflowing ashtray by his chair.

Apart from when she went up to Shropshire, Christine was generally quite chic. In the country she didn't wash her hair, and she wore jeans and some rather unpleasantly dirty running shoes. It was all a bit self-conscious, you see. She was a city girl. At work, and with all her media friends, Christine dressed expensively, in clothes that were purposefully plain and orphan-like. She was quite tall and she had an unusual face. The overall effect was definitely pleasing and she knew it. Rufus told Christine that she looked beautiful. She laughed and said, 'Steady on,' but she was pleased. At nine o'clock they left the flat and headed towards Notting Hill Gate.

Rufus and Christine arrived slightly late for dinner because they both had different addresses written down for their destination. Needless to say, Christine's was the right one. When they finally got there, the host and hostess greeted them with a most ridiculous amount of warmth. The BBC man and the magazine girl had secretly been frightened that Rufus and Christine would forget to turn up, so they clearly didn't know Christine at all.

Four of the six guests knew Rufus and Christine already and everyone was delighted to see each other. One of the girls (dressed in black – she worked on *Vogue*) had just written an incredibly witty and perceptive book about social spongers. Rufus had glanced at it in a bookshop the other day, and he'd felt his toes curling up with embarrassment for the writer, so he'd put it down. He turned to the Voguette and said:

'Christine's just been telling me about your book. Everyone's talking about it, it sounds wonderful. I'm afraid I haven't had the chance to buy it yet. But from all accounts I think I'll be on my way to Waterstone's first thing in the morning.'

The girl said, 'Oh wow, don't bother to *buy* it, it's an

37

absolute waste of money. Just take it to the lavatory next time you find it lying around in someone's flat.'

They laughed. The girl had lost a lot of weight since Rufus saw her last. Everyone else knew she was on some sort of drug, but poor Rufus didn't. She made him feel sick. He watched her picking at her food throughout dinner and disappearing to the lavatory soon afterwards. As the evening drew on, and Rufus grew drunker, he was totally obsessed by her. He thought he knew what he ought to do. Eventually he managed to draw her aside. He said:

'You've lost a lot of weight since I saw you last.'

The girl said, 'Oh wow, isn't it fantastic? I just seem to have lost my appetite entirely, the weight's just falling off me.'

Rufus felt sick, he felt a lump rise up in his throat. He didn't particularly like this girl, but he was very drunk and he remembered his guilt, and he understood his duty. He paused before he took such an ill-advised plunge. But he said:

'You should be careful. You should eat more. You're playing with fire.'

The girl looked as if about to interrupt him. She was rather offended. People didn't mention other people's habits. But Rufus bashed on:

'My sister just killed herself not eating enough. Don't think it'll just happen to someone else. It won't. It happened to her.'

The girl's face was a picture of compassion. She leant across and touched the top of his arm.

'Oh wow, I'm so sorry, you should have told me before. I don't know what to say. How incredibly grim. But I *swear* that's not my problem. I just don't have any hang-ups about my body.'

She laughed, then she looked awkwardly over Rufus's shoulder. She wanted to get away. This man was a weirdo, but she added:

'How absolutely awful for you. You must have suffered

terribly. How long ago did it happen?'

Rufus said, 'Oh not long,' but then he realised that he had to get out of the room. He was very drunk, and he was crying. He turned and stumbled towards the door.

Meanwhile Christine was flirting with the one man in the party she had never met before. When Lesley – their hostess – had invited Christine and Rufus to dinner, she had given them a run-down on the other guests. She said there would be a publisher and a lawyer, who it turned out Christine already knew, the Voguette who'd introduced the two couples to each other in the first place, and another female publisher who worked for a women's press and was actually quite nice. She was an old friend.

Then there was an Australian and his girlfriend. Lesley had only met them twice before. But the Australian was absolutely stinking – rolling in it. Lesley assured Christine that he would keep her laughing for a week. He was just too good and too rich to be true.

Anyway, that's who Christine was talking to, and she found him fascinating. In very anxious, drunken voices the two of them were discussing the problems of race relations in Australia, and to be honest neither of them had a clue what they were talking about. Christine was very earnest, she wanted to get to the bottom of it, but the millionaire Australian just wanted to talk about his last trip to San Diego.

When Rufus came back into the room nobody paid much attention. The thin girl was talking to the incredibly glamorous but gormless girlfriend of the Australian millionaire. The thin girl was pulling passionate faces about the Reagan/Nicaragua problem, and she was wearing a rather beautiful pair of Manola Blahnik shoes. The gormless girl, who hadn't even heard of Nicaragua and so didn't really feel in a position to comment on the political situation out there said, 'I love your shoes, are they Manola's?' and the Voguette, who was easily distracted from her cause, looked down at her feet.

'Oh, wow,' she said, 'aren't they *great*? You know I think Manola's a genius. He's just got such a distinctive style.'

'And he's such a *character*,' said the thick girl.

'Oh God, he's a *honey*.'

Then they talked about the Kenzo sale; there was an amazing coat that the thin girl has just been *praying* would be reduced. She was going in there tomorrow in her lunch hour to find out. The thick girl knew the coat and said she'd had her eye on it too. They would have to have a race to the shop to see who could grab it first.

Rufus watched them in silence. The names meant very little to him, although he had to admit he'd overheard Christine mentioning them in the past. He wondered who the girls thought they were impressing. And then he thought that really they knew they weren't impressing anybody. They were all taking part in some kind of competition, and they hadn't ever stopped to work out the prize, or even if there was one.

Rufus decided that he'd had enough. He wanted to go home. In fact he really wanted to go back to the country, maybe he was too old for London now. He looked at Christine; she seemed to be enjoying herself with the millionaire. But for once he decided that he didn't care, she would meet plenty more millionaires before she died and he was going to drag her away. He got up and called for Christine. She looked annoyed, but they left.

As soon as they got outside she went for him.

'Why the hell do you always have to get so bloody drunk? For Christ's sake, I was *ashamed* of you, ogling that stupid drug-addict all the way through dinner. What the hell did you say to her?' She didn't wait for a reply. 'You say you love me, and two seconds later you're making disgusting suggestions to a girl you've always claimed you thought was a creep. Sometimes, Rufus, I think I'm sharing my life with a stranger. It's about time you began to pull yourself together. I know you've had a bad time lately, but you can't accuse *me* of having been too demanding. And what do I get in return? A leering, hypocritical, incapable drunk. Your sister died two months ago now, and my patience is wearing a little bit thin and I don't think anyone would blame me for it. There are people worse off in this world than you, you know. Why don't you start thinking about them for a change?'

Rufus listened to this onslaught in hazy silence. At first he couldn't work out what on earth she was so upset about, and when he did, he really didn't want to explain himself. He'd realised by now that perhaps he'd acted a little rashly. He wouldn't want to see the Voguette again in a hurry – not that he would have done at the best of times anyway.

He mumbled, 'It's not what you think, although I can understand why it might seem that way. I'm sorry, Chris.'

Which was certainly *not* the best thing to say in the circumstances. Christine immediately launched into another attack. She couldn't bear being patronised – and especially by a man who couldn't even hold his drink, etc., etc. Rufus decided that it would be advisable to keep quiet, and to try and explain himself in the morning.

After a while, Christine, who you may have realised is a bit under the influence herself, found she was getting very little come-back from her loved one, so she stopped talking. They drove most of the way home in silence.

At breakfast the next morning, Christine grudgingly apologised for being a bit tough with Rufus the night before. Rufus said he was sorry for being so drunk and the two of them thought they were friends. They both had fairly mean hangovers that morning, and there was absolutely no question of discussing tactics for Shropshire until the evening.

Once Christine had left for work, Rufus took a cup of coffee up to his study and wrote a letter to his hostess of the night before to apologise for his drunkenness. Poor Rufus was in a terrible muddle, I'm *sure* that wasn't advisable, but he wanted to make amends to Christine and he didn't want to tell her about the ghastly conversation with the drug-addict Voguette.

Rufus wandered aimlessly around the house, looking at his watch every two and a half minutes. He had nothing to do, and the day was really creeping by. He wasn't in the mood to have lunch with any of his friends.

By tea-time Rufus had the brainwave idea of ringing his mother. It would be killing at least seventeen birds with one stone, it would please Christine, it would give him something to do, it would cheer up his lonely old mother and most importantly it would kill time until Christine got back.

So with a great deal of excitement, Rufus gathered up his cigarettes, an ashtray and a drink, and he rang home. Isobel wasn't in, which in a way was quite lucky, because Rufus always found it difficult to keep his mouth shut and he would have been bound to tell his mother about the plans for her beautiful Rectory. In his present frame of mind it was unlikely that he would have got his 'angle' dead right.

At last Christine came home. Rufus poured her a drink and they sat down. At work she had thought out the intricacies of her plan, and she was in very good spirits. Rufus was to go down to Shropshire first thing in the morning, and arrive at the Rectory unannounced in time for lunch – it would probably be quite a good idea if he took some food down with him. Over lunch and *no later*, Rufus was to tell his mother their plan, but he wasn't to make it seem too monumental. And then, when it came down to the nitty gritty, Rufus had to persist until he got his way. It was by no means a very good plan. For one thing it certainly didn't take into account Rufus's amenable character. But Christine was quite determined. She would ring up at about six and ask how it went. Then she would take the next train to Shrewsbury (taking still more days off work) and generally help to clear out the house before the builders came in. It was

February. Christine wanted to see the bed and breakfast open by July. Rufus pitied the contractors.

He took a taxi from the station, and this time he had enough money to tip the driver. Christine had seen to that. He walked straight into the kitchen and was surprised to see a strange young man – at least ten years his junior – sitting at the kitchen table eating a bowl of Shreddies. He wore a bathrobe that hung open to expose the front of his naked, hairless body. He seemed to be unaware of Rufus's presence, and Rufus watched him for a while as the stranger read the back of the cereal packet with extraordinary concentration. The sound of his chewing echoed around the room. It reminded Rufus of Anna at breakfast in the days before she refused to eat it. She used to drive him mad because she ate too carefully and too noisily.

Rufus said, 'Oh hello,' rather limply, and stood by the door waiting to see what would happen next. The young man moved his torso slowly in the direction of the voice, saw Rufus, and said, 'Hiya, how d'you get in?' He wasn't particularly interested; he turned his attention back to the Shreddies packet.

Rufus felt – understandably – a little irritated. 'I live here,' he said, 'How did *you* get in?'

The stranger put down his spoon and looked at Rufus with more interest. 'You live here? What, you mean . . . I mean . . . don't you mind that sort of thing then?'

Rufus felt cold. The man in front of him couldn't be more than twenty. He looked down at the stranger's exposed genitals and asked them, in a voice that was deceptively controlled, 'Where is my mother?'

'Your *mother*?'

'My mother.'

There was a pause; the young man thought he couldn't have heard quite right; 'Your *mother*?' He looked at first stunned, then relieved. 'Jeeeesus! how old does *that* make her?'

43

He laughed, a dirty, leering laugh and covered his lap with his dressing-gown. 'She's a randy old bugger for a granny,' he said. 'For a moment I thought you were her husband or something. I was calculating the odds of getting out of here alive.' He laughed again, and assumed that Rufus would join in with the joke.

Rufus could feel the anger rising up from the pit of his stomach. He took a step towards the young man and made as if to hit him. It was most out of character, but this man was *talking about his mother*.

Just then she walked in, bright-eyed and rosy-cheeked. She also was wrapped in a dressing-gown. She saw her son and she froze. Rufus saw his mother and he froze. The young man was still unaware of the atmosphere. He said:

'You never told me you were a grandmother,' and he laughed again.

Isobel didn't look at him. She said, 'I'm not . . . I'm not a grandmother.'

She was looking at Rufus.

At last the man felt uneasy. He stood up. 'Well, I'll be off then,' he said. 'I'll see you around sometime perhaps?' And as he passed her he took an awkward handful of her bottom. Rufus leapt forward, Isobel said 'No,' and the young man protected his face with his free arm. 'All right, all right, I'm going, OK?' he shambled towards the door and mumbled 'bunch of nutters' just loud enough for them to hear as he closed the kitchen door behind him.

There was a moment's silence. Rufus turned cold, un-comprehending eyes on to his mother.

'Well?' he said.

In his less emotional hours, Rufus had always been the first to advocate free sex for the unattached. His mother was lonely, he knew it, but the man could only have been twenty years old, and it was clear that the two of them barely knew each other's name, and – for Christ's sake –

this was his *mother*. No, this morning he had no room for compassion.

Isobel shrugged. Her head was bowed and her back was stooped. Suddenly she looked a hundred years old. Rufus felt no pity.

'Well?' he said again.

Isobel spoke, but she didn't look at her son. 'I'm sorry, Rufus, I never wanted you to know . . .'

'Know what?' he said. 'Do you do this sort of thing often? You make a habit of picking up young men a quarter of your age and then *seeing them around sometime*? Did you do it while Anna was alive, Mother, while she was upstairs resting?' Now that was below the belt. If you ask me it has nothing to do with him anyway. I only wish Isobel had had the spunk to tell him so.

But Isobel didn't seem to hear.

'I'm sorry, darling,' she said, 'you need never have known. I was lonely, Rufus, you have to understand that. It won't happen again, it's never happened before, I swear to you. We've always got on so well. Rufus, don't leave me. I was so lonely here in this big empty house. So lonely . . . no Anna . . . please forgive me. It hasn't happened for long . . .'

Rufus interrupted, he said it very quietly, 'Please, Mother, spare me the details'. He turned towards the door. No, he wouldn't leave her, but he had to get out of the house. 'Go and put some clothes on; I'll be back in an hour. I'm going to buy myself a drink.' He left, and Isobel stood silently watching him go. As he left the room, Rufus heard the front door bang. He paused; it must be the man leaving, and he didn't want to bump into him. He wanted a glass of whisky and he wanted to call Christine. He badly wanted to get out of the house.

He stood there, just outside the kitchen, in the room before the hall, and he waited.

Distantly he heard the sound of a starting car. He must

have parked at the back or he would have noticed it when he arrived.

The car drove away but still he stood there.

The house was absolutely silent and Rufus stood. From behind him he heard the clatter of a chair and a dull thud.

He waited.

He'd never known his mother to cry before. She never cried, but he heard muffled, monotonous sobs from the kitchen.

He didn't move, he listened to her tears and they meant nothing to him.

Isobel's misery grew louder, more passionate, more desperate. And then quite suddenly the noise stopped.

Silence again.

Rufus heard her chair scraped back against the kitchen floor, then he heard her *talking*.

'I'm sorry, darling. You must forgive me, I failed you and now I've failed your brother. You were a lovely girl . . . beautiful . . . too thin, always too thin. I've been a bad mother but you didn't have to die. Why did you die, darling? Now Rufus will die too, I suppose. That will be nice for you, darling, won't it? Rufus, you, your father, we're all dead really now. No, we couldn't have survived. I'm dead, you're dead and Rufus will die, oh yes, he'll die now . . .'

Oh Christ, she was completely mad.

Rufus moved, all thoughts of whisky gone from his mind. He stopped thinking of himself and he thought of his mother. He'd come down to help her. What was he doing?

He didn't want to look at his mother. He couldn't without thinking of her body. Of her upstairs . . . last night . . . this morning . . .

With a great deal of effort he forced himself to turn around, back towards the kitchen. He knew he couldn't leave his mother alone. Isobel heard the door open and immediately stopped talking. She stood and stared at her son, who was

46

standing stiffly in the far corner of the room. He wanted to keep the physical distance between them.

'I thought I'd have a drink here instead,' he said hopelessly. 'Why don't you go and get dressed? I've brought some lunch down with me from London. Christine sends her love . . . Look, go and get dressed, please, I hate seeing you like this. I've got something important to discuss with you. I'll cook the lunch.'

Isobel's pale, tear-stained face gazed in amazement at her son. She really thought she'd lost him for good. And a tiny bit of colour came back to her cheeks.

'All right, darling . . .' she paused. When she reached the kitchen door she turned around. 'And thank you, Rufus.'

Twenty minutes later Rufus had laid out the cheese and cold meat. He'd laid the table and he was sitting by the kitchen window with a drink in one hand and a cigarette in the other. He seemed to be calmer now. Isobel came in dressed much as she usually dressed. She too seemed more in control. Apart from her still-bloodshot eyes, the scene only half an hour ago might never have happened. Both mother and son knew that they would never mention the incident again. They were too alike. They would never forget it, but they would pretend to each other that it had never occurred.

Their conversation was rather awkward. They were polite to each other.

'What a delicious-looking lunch,' said Isobel.

'Yes, Christine bought it on the way home from work last night. She sends her love. Can I get you a drink?'

Rufus went away to fetch her a glass of vodka, and he thought of the strange man in his mother's bed – of the strange men in his mother's bed. He thought of his mother's orgasm. When their fingers touched as he passed her the glass, he quickly snatched his hand away. He wiped it on his trousers and turned his face to the wall.

Isobel felt his repulsion. Her voice was tight. 'So what

brings you back home? ... You said you had something important to discuss.'

He turned back to face her. 'I do, I do indeed, very exciting.'

'You're not engaged?'

'What? Oh no, much more exciting than that, but I'm not entirely sure how much you'll take to it.'

'Good Lord, Rufus, you must know me better than to think I'd be shocked by *that*.'

For a moment he looked bewildered, then he said, 'No, this has got absolutely nothing to do with me and Christine. This has got to do with *you*.'

'Oh. It's not money, is it?'

'Well, I suppose you could say that money comes into it, yes.' There was a pause. 'Listen, Mother' – he was warming to the theme – 'you said yourself just a minute ago that you were lonely, ya?'

Isobel flicked an imaginary piece of dirt off her incredibly grubby shirt-sleeve. 'I must say I do occasionally feel that the house is sometimes rather empty,' she said stiffly.

'And it's no good pretending, we both know that, well . . .' he paused again.

Isobel looked up, terrified of what he might say next.

'Well, that money's a bit short for you at the moment. Let's say you've overspent yourself.'

Isobel was never so relieved to talk about her finances.

'Christine thought that as you were alone in this big house, and you could do with the cash, that you might try to make a bit of money with it, I mean the house. You could open up a sort of hotel, only without a restaurant. You know, just somewhere where people – like travellers and things – could stay the night. It's such a pretty house, and think of all the interesting people you'd meet. Then you wouldn't have to rely so heavily on your art as a source of income, you could just paint when you felt like it. What do you think? I mean me

48

and Christine would help you out a lot at first, until you got into the swing of things, if you see what I mean. Christine says the council will give you a grant to do things up – and to mend the roof. It'd mean you could afford to go on living here. And I know you don't want to sell up any more than I'd want you to. What do you think?'

It mustn't be forgotten that Isobel's relationship with her son has been considerably weakened this morning. She wants to redeem herself. She thought earlier that she'd lost her son. Now he was talking about plans for her future in which he promises to play a leading role. She only half listened to what he had said. But right now she knew she wouldn't refuse him anything.

'Gosh,' she said, 'I've never thought of that. It's a lovely house, isn't it? I'm glad you love it too, you used to say it was too cold . . . I expect it's a good idea, Christine's usually right, but I'd need a lot of help and there's no reason why you should have to trouble yourself with it.'

Rufus interrupted. 'There's absolutely every reason why I should help. I just said I didn't want to see the house go out of the family. Where do you think I intend to raise my children when I eventually get around to having them? It's in my interest for you to be able to keep the house. I'd never be able to buy one anything like it.'

Rufus was surprised by his tact and his honesty. He saw his mother's face relax a little.

'Well, if you're sure then, I mean, I think it sounds like an exciting idea.'

Rufus didn't let her pause to think about the disadvantages of having her home gutted and modernised and taken over by strangers.

'Brilliant,' he said. 'I'll ring up Christine and tell her the good news, meanwhile, why don't you heat up that soup?'

He left the room feeling quite pleased with himself. He carried his heavy heart with him into the drawing room. And

49

his heart was still heavier than it had been when he woke up this morning, but for the moment there's no thought behind his sadness. It's been a constant burden; now it has a heavier presence. Rufus is young and resilient, I hope his luck improves.

He didn't tell Christine about what had happened that morning, and he knew he never would. Christine was so pleased by the news that she didn't seem to notice any change in her loved one's frame of mind. She said she'd be on a train that afternoon and that she was looking forward to seeing them. She had to go. She had a meeting with a very important client in ten minutes.

Rufus returned to the kitchen. He smelt the soup and he realised he was starving. They sat down to eat, and they almost relaxed. They discussed the plans for the Rectory.

'I think it's probably a good idea if the family have their own self-contained flat on the ground floor. It'd be a shame to lose the drawing room, don't you think? Now then, how many bedrooms, or rooms that can be converted into bedrooms are there in the house? *We* only need two bedrooms, one for you and one for me and Christine. If we have guests, then they can stay in the hotel bit. So that leaves us with seven rooms, plus we need a few extra bathrooms. And then there's Anna's room . . .' Rufus paused; he looked at his mother. 'I haven't been in there for ages.' He gave her some space. 'Do you think it'll be any good?'

Isobel said, 'No, no, no,' very quickly. 'That room gets terribly cold in the winter, and anyway it looks out over the back. I think we'd better leave that as a store room.'

Isobel had tried many times, but she still couldn't bring herself to clear it out. And now she didn't really want to. It stood as a kind of monument to Anna's memory. She didn't want her daughter to think there was no place for her here any longer. Anna's room had to stay as it was.

Rufus thought seven bedrooms was easily enough, so he

let it drop. But he thought Christine would have very little time for what she would see as Isobel's sentimentality and escapism. The room was bound to be converted eventually. He sighed. Sometimes Christine was a little bit too tough.

Mother and son sat over the debris of their lunch until it was time to fetch Christine from the station. Both of them pretended to the other that they were delighted with the plan, and they wondered whether the council would pay for a man to tidy up the years of chaos in the grounds outside. They wondered if the council would pay for central heating to be installed, etc., etc. But both of them knew they were talking a lot of fanciful nonsense, and that the action would really begin first thing in the morning once Christine had put on her running shoes and forgotten to wash her hair.

CHAPTER 4

BUT THEY UNDERESTIMATED her. Christine had changed into her running shoes on the train and she hadn't wasted a minute. It was half-past five when she arrived at Shrewsbury station. Too late, you might say, to get any serious business done that day. But Christine had already rung some local contractors from her office in London before she got on the train. They were due to come in the day after tomorrow (accompanied by various advisers and members of the council). That left Christine and the Burtons exactly one day and one evening to sort through and clear out thirty-three years of family clutter. Christine knew it would be painful for them, but she thought it would be all that much better if they did it in a rush; hanging around was always a mistake.

Isobel and Rufus greeted this piece of information with a forced enthusiasm, but their faces said differently. Christine saw, so she said:

'I know it's going to be difficult for you lot, but why do tomorrow what you can do today? Try and look at it with a positive attitude and you never know, it might turn out to be great fun!'

They certainly weren't sure about that, but they both nodded keenly and said, 'Oh yes, yes, yes, exciting . . . good to get things moving . . . shouldn't put things off,' etc., etc. They rambled on for a while and then Christine interrupted them. She rubbed her hands together.

'Now then. I thought possibly the best idea would be for us to split. Me and Isobel will start in the library, and Rufus you can begin with your own bedroom. I jotted down a few notes on the train coming up. As the house stands at the moment, we've got eight bedrooms, three bathrooms, five lavatories, four reception rooms (and your studio) and the big hall. Each bedroom will need a bathroom *en suite*, but I think five lavatories will do. We'll keep the kitchen, and one of the reception rooms – I'll leave that up to you Isobel, after all it is your house – and we need a bedroom and a bathroom for Isobel. When we come down, Rufus, we can stay in one of the guest rooms. How does that sound?'

But she didn't wait around to find out. She carried on:

'Now, I'm sure you've thought of a lot of trivial little changes that are going to have to be made too. Things like parking facilities – I talked to the contractors about that and they said they could deal with it. It's highly likely that the safety inspector will make us rewire the house. But we can think about those problems when we come to them. Right now we've got to get working. I suggest we have a late supper at the pub. Any questions?'

Rufus and Isobel looked at one another. Things were way out of their control now. There was a pause. Then Rufus said:

'Actually, I think you've miscalculated, there are only seven usable bedrooms in the house.'

Christine said, 'Nonsense, I've written a list. There's –' But Rufus interrupted:

'My mother and I think Anna's room wouldn't really be very suitable. It's too small and dark, and it gets very cold in the winter, and it looks out over the back.'

'Don't be silly, all the rooms get cold in the winter. We're going to have to install central heating all though the house. The view's fine, we can use it as a single room.'

Mother and son began to talk at the same time. He said, 'But that room is too dark,' and Isobel said, 'I don't think central heating would really *go* in there.'

Christine stopped what she was about to say. She looked at them.

'Now listen, I know that this could be a painful exercise for you. But it's no good doing a job by halves. Do we want to make a success of this venture or don't we? Are we really so immature that we're going to allow some sort of misplaced sentimentality to lead us to ruin? This house is going commercial, right? There is no part of it that's any more sacred or private than any other. I don't want to sound too harsh, I know things haven't been easy for either of you, but you can't go on pretending Anna's still with us. *She* can't use the room, and I'm sure she'd like to know that you were putting it to good use. I suggest me and Isobel clear it out first thing in the morning, when we're both feeling strong.'

Rufus and Isobel gave up. As long as they didn't have to do it this minute they felt safe. Perhaps they would be able to get out of it tomorrow. Maybe even the health inspector would say it was unfit for commercial use or something. They sighed and after as much dithering as they could get away with (which wasn't a great deal), they trekked off to change into working clothes. They worked hard that night. Christine said she wanted the bed and breakfast to have a country house 'lived-in' look, so she allowed Isobel to leave all the books on the shelves in the library. She was also allowed to take her most precious ornaments, etc., into what had been designated her part of the house. Isobel was forced to go through all her old drawers, and every now and then she found a letter from Rufus when he was at prep school, or an old picture of Adam teaching Rufus how to hold a gun. It was all terribly moving, but Christine said:

'Now then, you've got plenty of time to look at that later, right now we've got to get on.'

That evening Isobel didn't have the strength to argue. She was feeling her years, and it had been an unfortunate day.

By eleven o'clock they had, amazingly, cleared out about a third of the house. Christine was pleased with the day's work, but it was too late for supper at the pub. They ate breakfast cereal, and Christine talked and talked about work and the crowds in London and about how lovely it was to be in the country. Isobel and Rufus managed to laugh and agree in the right places, but their minds were elsewhere.

The next morning Christine woke them at six with a strong cup of coffee. She said the milkman had already been and that he'd left eggs and bread. She cooked them an enormous breakfast, and more or less forced them to eat it. She said they had a lot of work to get through that day, and that lunch wouldn't be till late. She was in her element.

The Burtons didn't have much of an appetite. Rufus was thinking of Isobel who was thinking about having to clear out Anna's room. She kept thinking of the jeans and the diary. She pushed her food around her plate, and Christine looked on disapprovingly.

Christine said, 'OK, Isobel, we've got a mean task ahead . . . keep your chin up, and when you're ready we'll go.'

Isobel tried to smile and she dropped her fork. She gave up her pretence of eating and just sat hunched, staring at her coffee.

Christine lit a cigarette. There was a pause; she said again, 'When you're ready.'

'I don't think I'm feeling very well,' Isobel said.

'Nonsense, you're feeling fine, you just haven't woken up properly. Take a last gulp of coffee and we'll set off.'

There was no escape. Isobel looked desperately around for Rufus's support but he had already been dispatched to start work in the red room.

Christine stubbed our her quarter-smoked cigarette impatiently and got up from the kitchen table.

'Come on,' she said in what she thought was a patient and compassionate voice. 'Once you've started it won't seem nearly so bad. It's like taking your driving test really.'

Isobel still sat, she still stared miserably at her coffee cup. Christine took a step towards her and leant her elbow on the table, so that their faces were level and very close. Isobel smelt the tobacco on Christine's breath and she felt sick.

'Look, you can't keep running away from the truth for ever. You've got to keep fighting, honey. You've got over the initial shock now, and if you haven't, then it's high time you did. I know you loved Anna, but keeping her bedroom isn't going to bring her back to life. You've got to look her death in the face. Anna's dead, and that's tragic, but life goes on. Now finish your coffee and let's get going, we haven't got much time.'

Isobel felt numb. She said, 'Don't call me "honey".'

Christine pretended not to hear. Actually, she was rather embarrassed. She'd thought it was rather an effective fond touch, and she was intending to make a habit of it. She waited and watched while Isobel pushed back her chair like an old woman. Christine marched towards the hall and Isobel tailed behind. She waited for her at the foot of the stairs, and she talked hard to keep Isobel's mind off things.

'You know, it occurred to me that this bed and breakfast will give you a perfect opportunity to exhibit your art. You could hang stuff all over the house and make it clear to everyone that the paintings are for sale.'

Isobel showed a tiny spark of enthusiasm.

They reached the threshold of the door and Christine paused. She half turned towards the mistress of the house, and she said, 'You do realise quite how necessary this is, don't you, love? I'm only so determined about it for you. It's your happiness I'm thinking of. Once this is done you'll feel much stronger for it; it's really long overdue.'

Isobel nodded and they opened the door.

'Good heavens, what a mess!' Christine made for the jeans immediately and without further ado picked them up and folded them. She'd brought a dustbin bag up with her. She said:

'I don't think I know anyone who'd be able to fit into these, it seems a shame, such a waste.' And she threw them in the bag. Then she looked at the unmade bed. 'Those sheets shouldn't be too dirty, we can probably just put them straight back into the linen cupboard.'

'Actually, I think they ought to be washed, you know,' Isobel said quietly. She put out her hands to take them and she caught sight of the diary again. She didn't want Christine getting her hands on that. She'd either force her to throw it away, or she'd decide it would be healthy to read it aloud as Isobel worked. She made a dive for the book.

'What's that?'

'What? Oh this – nothing, nothing at all, it's just a book I've been looking for for ages, I'd forgotten I lent it to Anna, I'll go right down and put it in the library.'

Isobel turned to go but Christine moved quickly. 'Oh no you don't, you can't get away as easily as that. For God's sake, this job has got to be done. I'm not bionic, so come on, the book can wait. Let's get moving.'

Isobel put the book just outside the door and prayed that it wouldn't be noticed. Christine decided that it was a waste to throw out all Anna's beautiful clothes, so they were put in a bag, and Isobel was instructed to take them to Oxfam the next time she went to Shrewsbury.

Isobel opened the top of Anna's desk. Anna had stuck a large and unflattering photograph of herself on the desk flap. She was wearing tight trousers and a sleeveless T-shirt. Isobel couldn't believe her daughter had ever had so much flesh. She really looked quite plump. Her thighs and the top of her arms bulged unattractively and the T-shirt was stretched across her chest. Isobel looked again and she felt sick. Anna had obviously used a penknife or a compass and she had scratched across the image of her smiling face. The marks were deep, you could see the wood of the desk top where half her mouth should have been. Isobel stared, mesmorised. There was a passionate self-hatred in the marks that she couldn't understand. Christine crossed the room and looked over Isobel's shoulder. She paused for a moment but not for long. She took Isobel's arm and led her to the bed.

'For a mother to be able to cope with something as horrendous as what you've just seen on that desk top, she has to be able to understand her daughter's frame of mind, and the motives behind what made her want to do it.'

Isobel wasn't listening.

'Your daughter was consumed with a hatred of herself that is very difficult for normal, sane people like you and me to understand. This is in fact what finally led to her unfortunate death. The photograph was evidently taken some time before Anna's decline. Actually she looks fatter than I ever remember her being. And she chose this picture for that very reason. She put it up there to horrify herself. It was a permanent reminder of what she saw as her old self. She probably thought she despised her old self even more than her "reformed" self – and mind, I put that in quote marks. Anna was a very disturbed child. This form of self-hatred is a classic expression or syndrome of her disease. I think you need to understand that. It was my intention that you should learn from this experience. It's vital that you have a clear idea of the disease that Anna died of. That way you will be stronger to work for the future.'

She'd finished and Isobel hadn't heard a word. She stared blankly ahead of her and thought of the deep etchings across her child's face. For the first time since she'd died, Isobel cried for her daughter. She cried silently, she sat quite still and allowed the tears to fall down her cheeks. Her hands lay limp by her side and the tears slid down her neck.

Christine got up from the bed. 'I'll do the desk if you like, I don't suppose you want to look at that picture again, do you?'

Apart from the photograph, the desk was in perfect order. Anna's cheque book lay neatly by her Mont Blanc fountain pen. There were some beautifully filed bank statements and some grand writing paper that she'd been given for Christmas about two years back. Then there was a photograph album that Christine had never seen before. She opened it – Rufus had been a sweet little boy.

But there were no pictures of Rufus inside, just pages and pages of the most incredibly intricate graph. Along the bottom axis were the dates – it started about two and a half years ago. Along the other axis were numbers beginning at nought and going up in fifties to four thousand – they were the calories. The line began with the first day when Anna had clearly eaten around a thousand calories, and then, apart from the occasional hideous jerks to right up above the 4,000 mark, it dropped steadily. Christine turned the pages quickly. The graph stopped about six months before Anna died, and by the end, the line was almost non-existent. About twice a week it rose above the nought axis, and then only to the 200 level at the highest. Isobel still sat on the bed; she didn't notice the unusual lack of activity behind her. Without looking up from the graph Christine moved back towards her.

'I think you ought to take a look at this,' she said. 'It will give you some idea of Anna's obsessiveness, and again, this is a typical syndrome . . .' She handed it to Isobel, or rather she put it on Isobel's lap.

'I'll explain it to you. This is quite simply a chart of Anna's food intake over the period of her illness – and it's interesting how long the illness had been going on before even *I* noticed . . .'

Isobel looked down at the book. Again she wasn't listening; the chart meant nothing to her. Anna had given up maths when she was fifteen, it was odd that this should still be hanging around. She pushed the book away from her lap and got up from the bed.

'I don't think it'll interest me very much, I've never had much of a head for figures. Thank you for being so helpful, I'm sorry to be such a trouble. I think I will go and lie down for a while, I'm not feeling very strong.' She left the room with a dignity and finality that even Christine couldn't argue with.

'I'll wake you up at lunch time shall I? I think a rest will probably do you some good. You do understand, I'm sorry to have to push you so much, but you understand don't you? The contractors are due in first thing in the morning . . .'

But Isobel had closed the door behind her. She remembered not to leave the diary behind.

Rufus and Christine worked hard, and the house was ready for the contractors by the time they arrived at nine the next morning. Christine locked herself up in the library with them for several hours and then she called Rufus. Together they gave the men a tour around the house.

It turned out that very few alterations had to be done. If the Burtons were prepared to pay overtime, which Christine said they absolutely were, then the bathrooms, the central heating and the general redecoration could be done in as little as eight weeks. They could start tomorrow.

Christine, who as I said before, was a lady of some means, decided that they couldn't hang around for grants from the council and bank loans, they could be sorted out later. She announced that she'd been thinking about it for a while (which wasn't entirely true) and that she was going to give the Burton family an interest-free loan until things were more settled. The Burtons could only say thank you.

Christine, who loved her her job in London, decided that the work on the Rectory would not be done properly or fast enough unless she was there to supervise it, and of course she was right. She rang up her office on Monday morning and asked to speak to the owner. She asked if she could take a three-month sabbatical. She knew that she'd taken a lot of time off lately, but she knew they knew that things had been difficult. She also knew that she was an asset to the firm and that it would be their loss if she left them.

The firm said she could take off two months and no more. Christine explained that she had to be there to organise the running of the bed and breakfast for a while, too. She couldn't possibly desert Isobel as soon as the building had been finished. They must be able to understand that. They didn't, so Christine gave in her notice. Very high-handed she was about it too, as well she could afford to be. She knew she'd get another job whenever she wanted. But she was still quite sad to leave – and she made that quite clear to her lover and his mother. They both felt very guilty, but there was nothing to be done.

Rufus had no real role in the activity at the Rectory (nor indeed did his mother). Christine said there was very little point in his staying down there wasting time when he could well be working on his book, so after a week hanging around uselessly at home he returned to London to hang around uselessly there.

Isobel and Christine were left alone in Shropshire, which was rather a strain for poor Isobel. The work on the house was actually ahead of schedule, but that was no thanks to Isobel. She spent most of her time forcing the workmen to take coffee breaks, and if Christine hadn't been there they would have been only too happy to oblige, but on the third day she noticed the trend so she called them all together and very tactfully (she understood what hard work theirs was) she told them that they were to have only one coffee break a day, and three-quarters of an hour off for lunch. They would have complained, as well they might, but none of them dared to argue with Christine, and she was very gracious.

The work moved fast, but Isobel didn't really see much of what was going on. After two days of being left almost entirely alone with Christine, she retired to bed. She said she'd been feeling unwell for some time and that she was sure it was only exhaustion. Christine argued that she didn't see quite what it was that had made Isobel so exhausted, she'd led a very peaceful past few months – or even years – but Isobel wouldn't hear.

The work was finished in just under two months, and apart from at weekends when Rufus came down, she refused to come out of her bedroom. Her meals were brought upstairs to her and were left largely untouched outside her bedroom door. She didn't want to be disturbed.

She lay in bed, surrounded by photographs of her dead husband and her dead daughter. She looked at pictures of them on the lawn, in the library, on the tennis court, in the days when the house was at its most splendid, and she listened to the whistling workmen with their chisels and hammers and saws and drills. She had no curiosity about what they and her future daughter-in-law might be doing to the house. She lay and only wanted to remember the way things used to be. For the first time in those days, she saw clearly how her life was falling apart. And for the first time she understood how she and she alone was responsible for it.

She never opened the diary although she spent hours stroking its covers and wondering if she could, but she knew she never could. Isobel wasn't nosy, she didn't want to know about Anna's sex life or her fantasies, she just wanted to try and understand her, to understand what made her daughter inflict what she did on her family. But she would never forget the vandalised picture in Anna's desk, and she knew she did not want to have to cope with any more revelations of that kind.

Actually, she was frightened of the diary. She would have thrown it away, she wanted to, but somehow it stuck to her hand.

About three times a day Christine knocked on the bedroom door, but Isobel pretended to be asleep. At first Christine used to wake her and force her to show an interest in what was going on, but she was met with such a frosty, sleepy reception that eventually she took the hint and gave up. For all her attempts to improve poor Isobel's financial situation, she must have run up an enormous telephone bill. She told her friends that she enjoyed the unusual solitude, that it gave her time to think things out, but in fact she was bored, and she was itching to get back to London and to her Voguettes and Australian millionaires. A month was the longest period of time she'd ever spent alone in the country. Her former fantasies of eventually retiring there were shattered.

★   ★   ★

So the day came when the house was ready for guests. They had advertised in the local papers and glossy magazines for the past month, and the first guests were due to arrive Saturday lunch-time. Oh, but the house was in a fever of excitement. Isobel had risen from her bed, as she always did when Rufus came down, and she had washed her shirt. She was wearing a skirt and she looked quite sparky-eyed. Christine was marginally irritated by her miraculous recovery – just when the action started.

Rufus kept striding with great purpose towards the hall; he said some hinges had to be oiled. Anyway, he found himself several manly tasks to while away the morning. Christine spent the morning in the cash and carry. She bought three bulk-sized tins of Nescafé, fifteen loaves of ready-sliced white bread (they could be frozen), a ridiculous amount of bacon and eggs, and endless other bits and pieces that the English seem to find it necessary to eat at breakfast time.

She got back to the Rectory at around one, and she cooked some pasta which she added to some pre-heated Buitoni pasta mix and she and the Burton family ate it, saying all the while how extraordinary it was that a sauce could be so good when it only came out of a tin.

'The Italians are so clever, it's no wonder English food is so nasty,' said Rufus. It didn't make much sense, but nobody seemed to notice, they weren't really thinking about the Italians at all.

At last the doorbell rang (Rufus had checked it worked earlier this morning), and the three of them sprang up. Christine opened the door.

There stood a young, unattractive, quiet-looking couple, dressed quite clearly in their rather dismal Sunday best. They'd failed to mention that this would be their honeymoon night. Christine knew they were off to Spain early the next morning, but the person who'd booked the room had had such a dull middle-aged voice that any idea of romance hadn't come into her head.

They both looked very happy, rather shy and deeply in love. It was quite clear. Christine said:

'Oh, goodness, do come in, I'm afraid you're our very first guests, so we're all feeling rather nervous. But everything's strictly under control, don't worry about a thing . . .'

'It's a shame the roof's just caved in,' said Rufus. The Burton faction roared with laughter. Then Christine said:

'Well, now we've broken the ice, why don't you come into the drawing room and we'll have a celebratory cup of tea.'

'Have you been married long?' said Isobel. She thought

64

that under the circumstances the last thing the happy couple would want right now was a celebratory cup of tea with the Burtons.

'Well, in fact we've just got married this morning. We came straight from the reception,' said the man. He looked at the girl and they both giggled.

'Good heavens,' said Christine, 'then the last thing you'll be wanting to do is drink tea with us lot. I'll show you your room immediately, and if you want anything, then just holler.' She gave a crude laugh and everyone looked at the carpet. The couple looked at the carpet too, but they giggled, and they tripped behind Christine as she led them upstairs. They talked in whispers and they giggled behind her. Christine told them again that they were the first guests to be staying at the Rectory, and then she told them about the problems the family had had in installing the central heating, and that the house used to be very cold in the winter.

She unlocked their door and threw it open proudly. She stood back and waited for admiring comments, but the couple didn't even look away from each other's lovely faces.

Christine was annoyed and hurt. 'I hope you enjoy your stay with us,' she said, but she wasn't acting or feeling like her usual self. She was furious; they were incredibly common and they'd treated her as an inferior. If they only knew how smart and grand she was . . . she marched back down to the drawing room and when she got there she sat down. For the first time she had no instructions to give and really nothing to do.

CHAPTER 5

So The Weekend passed and the honeymooners left. But more guests were expected and more guests came and went. The Rectory began to get quite a name for itself, what with the really weird householders and the really nice atmosphere. The Burtons continued to advertise and within two weeks of opening at least three rooms were booked up every day for the next three months. Christine was a tremendous help. In fact she did more or less everything. Well, as yet they didn't have any outside help, and poor respectable spoilt Isobel couldn't see that *she* was expected to change honeymooners' sheets and empty retired majors' ashtrays (yes, there were a lot of them).

Isobel did cook the breakfast, she enjoyed that. And she showed the more interested guests around the house. Sometimes she quite shocked herself, because she put a lot of energy into making it clear to the gentle tourists that she *was* rather grand after all. There was a portrait of Adam's great-great-grandfather who'd been a Lord Mayor of London, and there was a carpet that was said to have come from Versailles. Really, the hotel was just a hobby.

Christine listened to Isobel giving her guided tours and she thought Isobel might be being a bit vulgar, but she never mentioned it. She wouldn't exactly have liked Isobel to stop. Anyway, it gave a certain character to the hotel. People would remember their stay there and talk about it once they'd left.

So Christine's been incredibly unselfish. She doesn't enjoy changing people's sheets, and by now she's dying to get back to London. Apart from anything else, she misses Rufus, but her conscience has told her to stay with Isobel until things are more sorted out.

On the fourteenth day of its opening, the Old Rectory Hotel, as it was imaginatively called, received a booking that made Christine quite confident of its financial future. A retired schoolmaster and his wife rang to ask if the hotel took permanent residents. Christine took the call and actually it hadn't occurred to her, but by now you know she's a very decisive woman, so she said yes immediately.

'I think we might even be able to give a small reduction, seeing as you're buying in bulk,' she said.

The schoolmaster laughed and thought that Christine sounded like a very sporting girl. He made an appointment to come with his wife and look around. He asked for directions about how to get there from London. That was almost Christine's favourite bit. She said things like, 'You take the M54 and leave it at Junction 7. Turn left off the A5 just after a rather pretty Norman church . . .' The schoolmaster took careful notes and thought that he and the *maîtresse de maison* would get along fine. He said he was looking forward to meeting her and then Christine went off to tell the good news to Isobel.

It was time to sort out the problem of help. Christine was planning to return to London very soon now, but she couldn't go before they found someone to make the beds. Christine thought it would probably be better if the employee lived in. The hours were difficult and anyway that way there would be no calling off sick or general skiving.

She knew more or less what she wanted, it was on the au pair girl lines. They were by far the cheapest. She wanted a young girl who needed a roof above her head and a bit of pocket money to spend on cigarettes. She had to be pretty. Much though it went against the grain, Christine was forced to admit that ugly girls didn't attract customers, and she couldn't let her politics get in the way. She was running a business here.

In a muddled sort of way Christine also thought it would probably be good for Isobel to have a young girl about the house anyway. Since Anna died Isobel had seen very few, in fact she seemed almost consciously to avoid them. And that was no good at all. Unhealthy. Isobel couldn't be allowed to cut out any section of society from her awareness.

So she took Isobel aside after dinner one night to discuss it, or rather Isobel was told of Christine's decision and she reacted quite positively. She'd been dreading the idea of making beds, and even the breakfasts were beginning to pall. (But on the few occasions that she's allowed to, Isobel still likes taking bookings, and she loves the guided tours.)

Anyway, the discussion was a short one. Christine said she would advertise for a young girl and she would interview everyone who applied. She promised Isobel that she wouldn't return to London before someone suitable was found.

★　　★　　★

A week later Christine sat importantly behind Isobel's desk in the drawing room. She had some clean file paper in front of her and a typed list of questions specially designed to get to the bottom of every applicant's soul.

It was nine o'clock and Isobel had been dispatched on an errand in Shrewsbury. Isobel did things pretty slowly, and Christine calculated that it should keep her away until lunch, by which time Christine would have interviewed all the girls, made her decision and got them out of the house. She thought Isobel would be bound to make a nuisance of herself in one way or another, and if she saw any of the applicants she would immediately fall for the most obviously unsuitable.

In the hall, where Christine had put seven chairs in a neat row the night before, there sat seven fairly middle-class girls between the ages of seventeen and twenty-two, dressed in sensible corduroy skirts and Benetton jerseys. They all looked pretty ill at ease and they sat with their hands in their laps looking at the paintings in silence until the dog wandered in. And as Christine would say, that 'broke the ice'. Then they called the dog over and patted it and told each other about the pets they had at home. The conversation heated up and they began to make a certain amount of noise.

Inside the drawing room Christine heard and for some reason she was rather annoyed. She'd wanted to keep the atmosphere fairly tense to keep the girls on their toes. Christine has some unattractive sides to her otherwise commendable character.

There had been fifteen answers to Christine's advertisements. She'd made the job sound marginally more attractive than it actually was. The other eight applicants couldn't even be considered, mostly because they were too old. One woman had said she had two children and no man and could she bring them too. Christine thought seriously about that one. She rather liked the idea of helping struggling single parents. But she was running a business not a charity. The woman really wasn't her problem.

As the noise from the hall grew louder, Christine realised she was ready to talk to the first applicant. She took out the appropriate letter and reread it; she sighed.

Dear Madam,

With great excitement I glanced upon your advertisement for being assistant manageress in your new hotel. This sounds like a super job and I was most pleased and pleasantly surprised when the advertisement went on to say 'no experience required'!!

I will tell you something about myself. My name is Sarah Cookson and I am eighteen years of age. I left school after taking A levels during which time I enjoyed the responsibility of being a prefect and captaining the second eleven girls' hockey. Fortunately I do have experience of hotel management and the catering business as I was lucky to do cookery A level whilst I was at school and I enjoyed the course enormously! Ultimately I would like to own and run my own country hotel, and I feel that this is an excellent opportunity to gain some experience in that area.

I enjoy meeting people and I'm certainly not afraid of hard work!! I enjoy talking to children and old people whom I find very interesting. During my time at school I spent several afternoons doing voluntary services, and I'm still a familiar face at our local home for old folks!

It would be super if you found the time to talk to me about it further and in this instance I will be able to tell you more about myself! I am fully available at the above address at all times.

I look forward to hearing from you!

Yours sincerely,

Sarah Cookson

Oh God, well she certainly seemed to have enthusiasm for the job, but Christine thought that poor Isobel was going to have to spend a great deal of time with her. They would have to eat together. Still, Christine reminded herself once more she was running a business, not a comedy show. She put the letter down and moved towards the door leading to the hall.

'Well, you all seem to have made yourselves quite at home already. I'm sorry to have kept you waiting so long. I would offer you coffee but time's rather short and you can see there is a lot of work to be got through this morning.'

70

The girls tittered politely and waited for instructions. Sarah Cookson was called for, and the rest of the girls fell silent again as they watched poor Sarah gather up her coat and bag and follow Christine as she strode back towards the drawing room.

'Do sit down.'

'Thank you.' Sarah cleared her throat and straightened her skirt. She looked up at Christine in what she thought was eager anticipation.

Christine lit a cigarette and offered one to the girl.

'No thank you. I don't smoke.' It was a bad start.

'Now then, you say you did cookery A level, but you didn't mention your grade, not of course that that's of the utmost importance, but I don't like to be led astray. Did you actually *get* the A level?'

'This is correct. The thing was, the nutrition tutor and I had a character clash, we couldn't get on, and I had a lot of personal problems at the time which I won't go in to . . . My boyfriend . . .'

'So you don't actually *have* a cookery A level, is that right?'

'This is correct, but as I say, I had a lot of personal problems at the time which are more or less sorted out now. I needed to get away from things at home, which is why this job is so ideal.'

Christine asked her a few more questions. The girl would not possibly do, but after all she'd made a long journey to get there. Eventually Christine managed to persuade her that willing though Christine was to give Sarah a job, it was just too bad that the girl had decided she wanted to stay with her family in London.

They parted company on the best of terms and Christine called the second interviewee in.

Outside, the others asked Sarah how it went.

'Oh she's ever so nice, you know, she says what she thinks which I really admire, but in fact I don't think the job's really for me and she was ever so nice, she said she thought I'd be right for it, but I wasn't really cut out for the country. And it never really occurred to me but I think she's right really. I'd get really bored, I mean there aren't very many young people here . . .' She talked about herself for a little longer and the girls began to lose interest.

Sarah noticed a rather tired, thin girl sitting on the edge of the group. She wasn't patting the dog or talking about her boyfriend with the rest of them. She was just watching and looking ill at ease. Sarah didn't want to catch the bus back to the station by herself, she was going to have to hang around until the others were ready to leave, so she moved in.

She sat down beside the thin girl and with very little ado, began to pour out her problems. Not only was her boyfriend two-timing her, but she had very bad period pains. The thin girl wasn't really listening, but she looked distantly sympathetic until her turn came in the interview room.

★   ★   ★

Inside the drawing room Christine was gradually becoming more and more despondent. She'd interviewed four of the seven girls and they were all as dull and limp and spoilt as each other. She caught herself wondering what was the matter with the younger generaton and that made her furious.

★   ★   ★

Outside, Sarah was pretty pissed off with the lack of come-back she was getting from the thin girl. She'd just said her parents were going through a divorce and the thin girl had looked blank and said, 'Oh really.' Some people were so heartless. She tried another tack.

'With my last boyfriend I used to get really bad cystitis, but then I went to the clinic and it seems to have got a lot better now. A friend of mine got VD once but she was such a little slut I think she deserved it. Some people just don't have any respect for their bodies, they'd just go to bed with anybody. I only go to bed with somebody if I really love them. How many men have you slept with, Katie?'

Poor Katie thought it was a little premature in their relationship to be discussing things like that. Anyway, she couldn't bear talking about sex at the best of times. She looked at Sarah, who was looking at her, and still waiting for an answer. There seemed to be no escape. Katie opened her mouth and tried to think of something evasive to put her interrogator off the scent, but she needn't have bothered. Sarah was much more interested in counting up her own list of sexual conquests.

'I lost my virginity on my fifteenth birthday, that was with David, he was really special to me. We're still really close friends now, he's like a brother really, I tell him everything . . .'

Katie was finding this all very difficult. She found herself staring longingly at the drawing-room door. Once she thought she saw the doorknob turn and she felt almost dizzy with relief. But Sarah kept on.

'Then I went out with Michael and I could tell he really respected me. He was a really thoughtful lover. We don't see each other any more. You know, we really cared for each other but we knew it would never work . . . if you don't mind I still find it very painful to talk about . . .'

The drawing-room door opened and Katie leapt to her feet. Christine stood in the hall and she looked down at a piece of paper in her hand.

'Melanie Matron, please,' she said, 'and then I think there are only two of you left, is that right? I'm sorry to keep you all waiting like this. In about half an hour I'll drop you all at the station, OK?' She looked up distractedly and without waiting for any replies she turned back into the drawing room.

Katie sat back down again. She was beginning to feel quite

73

seriously angry with poor Sarah. But what could she do? There was no escape. If Katie had been a more relaxed, easy-going sort of girl, then she would have found the whole thing rather funny, but she was very hyped up about this job. It really was quite important that she got it. And she hated people who talked about sex. Sex really wasn't her thing.

'Hello, Melanie, thank you so much for coming all this way. Do sit down.' Christine had changed her approach. 'So tell me a bit about yourself. You say in your letter that you left school two years ago. What sort of things have you been doing since then?'

'Well, you see, so far I haven't really found a job that's suited me. Basically I've been at home doing odd jobs for the family. I always used to cook my little brother's tea and that was quite good fun, so I've had a bit of experience really.'

'I see. What made you apply for this job in particular? Is there any reason why it's likely to suit you any more than any other?'

'Well, no, not really. But Dad found the advert and I think he's getting a bit fed up of me hanging around at home. He says I ought to go out and build a life of my own or something. Mum didn't really like the idea, but Dad said he'd pay for my fare up here and for my next three driving lessons if I gave it a try, so here I am.'

Christine sighed. 'All right, I think that's all now. Thank you very much, Melanie. You and all the other girls will be hearing from me in the near future. Could you send in Katie Dye for me, please?'

Melanie looked rather surprised and disappointed. She was just settling down to a comfortable conversation about herself. She wondered where she'd gone wrong. Or maybe she hadn't gone wrong at all and the woman had already decided that she was the right one for the job. Melanie only half liked the idea. Of course it was flattering. But she didn't want to move away from her family, and to be honest she didn't really want

74

a job. She thought she was quite happy with her life. She couldn't understand what her father was fussing about.

Anyway, she got up from the chair that she'd barely sat down in and said:

'Yeah, OK, it was nice to meet you. I like your house.'

Christine laughed. It was a shame, she rather liked Melanie Matron. She had a certain simplicity about her – and a wonderful name.

Melanie came out into the hall.

'Katie Dye?' she looked around casually and Katie jumped up again.

'Your turn. Watch out, she's a real bitch.' Melanie found it very difficult to be pleasant about anybody once she'd left their company and that, once you got to know her, was part of her charm. People always flattered themselves – and Melanie was the first one to encourage it – that they were the one exception to the rule. Almost everyone believed they were her best friend, but they were all terribly wrong.

So Katie, who was all of a dither anyway, felt her whole stomach heave when she heard what Melanie said. She would have liked to ask for more details, but there was no time and anyway her mouth felt dry and she had to concentrate on solving that between her chair and the drawing-room door.

Sarah said, 'Good luck! I promise you, you'll need it!' and wondered if she could attract the attention of the girl who'd just come out.

Sarah was one of those irritating girls who always re-membered people's names and insisted on using them at every opportunity and more. She said:

'How was it, Melanie?' and she didn't wait to listen for the answer. Within seconds she was talking about her period pains again. And this time she was getting a bit more come-back. Melanie had bad period pains too and when she was fourteen her mother had put her on the pill and she hadn't looked back since. She gave a crude laugh and Sarah was disappointed. Honestly, how could people have such an animal attitude to something that was so beautiful?

Katie knocked on the door and waited. She heard a muffled (self-important) 'Come in', so she did. The woman at the desk didn't look up and suddenly she thought she was back in her headmistress's office. Katie made the long walk from the door to the desk and she stood awkwardly in front of Christine and waited to be asked to sit.

Christine was play-acting. She still didn't look up, and Katie thought, 'My God, she really *is* a silly bitch, who the hell does she think she's impressing anyway?' She coughed. Christine put down her pen and slowly raised her head.

When Christine saw the girl she just stared. Her mind was racing, why on earth hadn't she thought of it before? This was exactly what Isobel needed to bring her back to life. Of course it would be hard to accept at first, and it was certainly a gamble. If it paid off, then the Burton family would live happily ever afterwards, but if it didn't . . . Oh God, did she dare? Was it really worth the risk? Christine still didn't say anything. She sat there frozen, just looking and working out odds.

The girl shifted her negligible weight to the other foot and ran her fingers through her thinning hair. What had she done, what was the matter with this woman? Katie thought she ought to say something. She said:

'Hello, the last girl said it was my turn . . . I'm Katie Dye . . . you know, about the job. Shall I sit down?'

Christine collected herself. 'Of course, I'm so sorry, you just reminded me of someone I used to know. It was a bit of a shock, that's all. Please, sit down.'

Katie sat; there was another pause and Christine carried right on staring.

'I've never been to Shropshire before, it's a beautiful county . . .'

Christine wasn't paying attention, 'Yes, yes, it is, isn't it?'

76

God, what was *with* this woman? Was she some kind of *lesbian* or something?

Christine tried to take control of the situation. She'd decided she wanted the girl. It really didn't matter, anyone could be trained to do a bit of housework. But she didn't want the girl to guess, she had to carry out a normal interview.

'So tell me a bit about yourself, Katie. You come from London, don't you? Whereabouts in London do you live?'

'Well, at the moment I'm living in a hostel in Victoria, but it's incredibly expensive, and I'm going to have to find somewhere else pretty quick before they kick me out. I haven't paid the last two weeks' rent.'

Christine, so hard and businesslike, thought: Oh good, that means she's pretty desperate. She can't pick and choose. Perhaps if we say we'll pay the rent she's owing, she'll agree to start immediately.

'So you don't live with your family any more?'

Katie's face changed. She looked quite sad and quite hard.

'No, we fell out a little while back. They live in Berkshire.'

Christine thought, this is getting better and better.

'Do you have a job at the moment, Katie?'

'Um, no, no I don't, but you can see I'm trying.'

'You're very thin, it looks like you need a bit of feeding up.'

'Yes, it would be nice to get a job out of London. London's so dirty, isn't it?'

Sensitive Christine took the hint and learnt what she needed to know. She said for the sake of it, 'Have you had any experience in this line of work before? Or perhaps you did cookery at school? You didn't tell me very much about yourself in your letter. Have you got any particular ambitions? Tell me all!'

Katie's tight little mouth began to open and close. She was telling a bit, but she certainly wouldn't tell all. Christine

77

wasn't listening. She watched the gaunt face moving and she looked into the hollow, tense, even shifty eyes. Christine didn't need to listen, really she knew all she needed to know about this girl already. She recognised the shifty eyes and the thin, thin hair and the swollen glands. She'd seen the repulsive thinness somewhere else.

I shouldn't need to tell you, and if you haven't understood by now, then I'd prefer it if you put this book away. Katie was ill. Katie was another anorexic.

'. . . so you see the only jobs I've ever really had are wait-ressing ones . . .'

Katie's voice tailed limply away. She waited for the next set of questions. But Christine thought she'd wasted enough time already.

'That's fantastic! You're just what we're looking for. When can you start?'

Katie looked amazed. She was delighted. 'You mean I've got the job? Just like that?'

'Just like that,' said Christine smugly. She really ought to have been a teacher.

'Well today, tomorrow, any time you want me. I've just got to fetch my things from Victoria, and I'm yours! God,' she said. She grinned and somehow it looked grotesque on her miserable, obsessive little face. 'I just can't believe my own luck.'

Christine thought that under the circumstances she needn't even bother to bribe the girl by offering to pay her outstand-ing rent. Unless it proved to be a difficulty, then Katie could sort that out herself. She'd forgotten it for a while, but Christine was running a business here, not a foster home for mixed-up teenagers.

'Right then, Katie, let's get a few things straight.'

Katie looked slightly taken aback, she wasn't used to such forthrightness.

'I'm not actually the person you'll be working for.'

Christine was about to explain her relationship to Katie's future boss when she realised how ridiculous it would sound. So she stopped what she was saying and felt slightly put out. Yes, she was going to have to work on Rufus next, it really was about time. Instead she said:

'Mrs Burton's out at the moment, but I'm sure you'll both get along very well . . . She's an artist. Do you have any interest in art?'

'Oh well, I was going to go to art school . . .'

Christine interrupted, she wasn't interested. She looked at her watch. Isobel might be back at any moment. She had to get Katie out of the house before then at all costs.

'Now, you know this is a very new business and as it stands we obviously can't pay you an enormous salary. But depending on what you yourself put into the hotel, and of course depending on our final profits, we may in a few months be able to give you a raise. We'll give you free board and lodging and one day off a week. So whatever you are paid would of course be pure pocket money. You will be treated like one of the family and be expected to eat with Mrs Burton in the kitchen unless you have something better to do. Mrs Burton is the owner of the house and you will be working directly beneath her – and indeed *only* with her. You are the sole employee of the Old Rectory Hotel.'

Katie thought Christine was sounding pompous, and now she realised that she'd got the job and Christine wasn't the boss, she thought she could afford to make a joke.

'Good heavens, how grand!'

Christine stopped what she was about to say and looked patiently at the new employee.

'Now look, Katie, if we're just going to be frivolous about this . . .'

'Oh, no, no, please, I'm not being frivolous at all. I just didn't realise there was so much responsibility . . . which is brilliant, I'm really excited, please, carry on.'

'Right then. How does twenty-five pounds a week sound to you?' Christine said grandly.

Katie's face fell and she tried to hide it. She had to have this job, she just couldn't afford to carry on living in London, and anyway she hated it there, but twenty-five pounds a week was pretty bloody mean. It wasn't as if the family could be short of it in a pile like this, with all these antiques and paintings and things. Katie knew that if she accepted the tiny salary now then she'd be furious for it later. She thought she'd risk it.

'I don't suppose you could stretch it to thirty could you? I mean, I've got one or two debts that've got to be paid off eventually.'

Christine was surprised. She'd misjudged this girl. Before the interviews began, Christine had calculated on paying between thirty-five and forty a week, but when she saw how desperate Katie had looked, she thought she'd probably be able to get away with a lot less. She was slightly annoyed, she didn't like being argued with.

'As as I say, this is a young and struggling business. How big are your debts?'

Katie exaggerated. 'About three hundred.'

Oh wow, Christine thought, nothing! But she was running a business so she said:

'OK, what say you we pay off your outstanding debts immediately and you still start at twenty-five?'

Katie felt she couldn't argue. If only she knew how badly Christine wanted her, she might have been able to stretch it to a hundred.

'That sounds great. When shall I start?'

'On Monday. That gives you a week to sort things out. I'll write you a cheque for fifty now, and I'll give you the rest later. I'll just have to give the last girl a quick interview so she doesn't think she's come all this way for nothing, and then I'll drop you all off at the station. You don't seem the talkative type, but anyway I think it'd be wiser if you kept mum to the rest of them that a final decision's already been made. I'll look forward to seeing you on Monday. Ring and tell us what train you'll be on.'

They shook hands and Katie almost skipped to the door.

In the hall Melanie and Sarah seemed to be getting on like a house on fire. Melanie was telling Sarah some really gory details about her elder sister's experiences with childbirth, and Sarah was talking over her. She was saying that another friend who was like a brother to her had announced he was homosexual and that she thought that was all right, people were so narrow-minded and she and the boy in question were still really good friends. Mind you, she thought twice about shaking his hand or anything, what with the AIDS scare and all that.

Katie listened to them agreeing with each other and decided that, of the two, she preferred Melanie, but that they were both pretty ghastly.

She turned to the last girl to be interviewed. She hadn't moved from the seat she was allocated to three hours before, and she was *still* patting the dog. Katie didn't mind that the girl had wasted her time and money coming all the way up to Shropshire from wherever it was she lived.

'Your turn.'

The girl looked up, but she left her mouth open. She stared at Katie.

'Pardern?'

'I said it was your turn to be interviewed.' Katie said it rather irritably.

The girl stared at Katie for a couple more seconds before she could take in what had been said to her. She still didn't close her mouth.

'Oh . . . thanks.' Very slowly she picked up her bag and dripped towards the door. And that is the last that we or Katie will ever see of her, which is a blessed relief.

81

CHAPTER 6

ONLY TWO MONTHS before her interview at the Old Rectory Hotel, Katie Dye still lived at home. Her father, who came from quite seriously humble origins, had made a substantial amount of money in insurance, or contract building or fast food. Anyway, he was very rich, and he'd definitely *risen* in the world. That was wonderful. Katie had never wanted for anything. Her wardrobe was the envy of the upper sixth, and so were her video recorder and her enormous television and the brand-new car she'd been given on her seventeenth birthday. Katie was pretty and clever and rich. It really did seem like the world was her oyster, and maybe that was the problem.

Mrs Dye was a naturally slim woman some years her husband's junior. She had very little to do with her days, so she spent most of them buying Valentino jackets and smoking extra-long cigarettes and finding lovers. Her lovers were all pretty similar and although she tried her hardest not to be, she was a stupid woman and she was most indiscreet. The only person who never seemed to hear of her infidelities was her husband, who was too busy making money and doing the same himself.

Kind girls at school, whose parents moved in the same society as the Dyes, used to find it was their duty to pass on any idle gossip to their only daughter. Katie used to pretend to laugh and make half-baked jokes about the mid-life crisis. But she kept it all to herself and she minded very much indeed.

Mr Dye treated his lovers in much the same way that most of Mrs Dye's lovers treated her. The men bought the women silken knickers and expensive jewellery and took them out to places like Tante Claire for dinner. They thought they were living a most daring and glamorous life, but they were all bored. I mean, nobody was really *achieving* very much.

At some point, when even the pretence of excitement has gone from cheating on each other, the Dyes are bound to get a divorce, but they were still together – in a manner of speaking – when Katie left home two months ago. Katie hadn't wanted to leave home. But she pushed her luck too far and the Dye parents, who it can be seen were a pretty selfish and ignorant couple, had no understanding or patience for their daughter's adolescent neurosis. Eventually they turned her out of the house and told her never to darken their doorstep again.

To be honest, and I have very little to say in defence of her parents, Katie did behave quite badly – quite madly.

I'll tell you how it happened.

* * *

Katie always used to be the favourite of her teachers and the leader of the gang. When she was fifteen she used to be able to laugh and flirt and dress better than any of her contemporaries. She never seemed to do any work but she always did well in exams. And she was always at the centre of the troublemakers, but it was always her friends that got caught. Life, you might say, couldn't have been rosier.

At about the same time Mrs Dye told her daughter that she was pregnant. Katie said she was pleased. After all, she was quite grown-up now, and she'd had fifteen years of being an only child. It occurred to Katie that Mr Dye might easily not be the new baby's father, but being a sensible girl, she kept her wicked thoughts to herself. And it would have been fine if only a few jealous people at school hadn't found it necessary to wonder aloud whether the father of her future sibling was Mike, the local hotelier, or Mr Winchape, the local insurance broker.

Her friends said, 'Just ignore them, they're only jealous.' And poor Katie tried her damnedest.

Anyway, nine months later Mrs Dye was delivered of a little boy, and during that time Katie began to lose weight. But her best friend was still thinner than she was, and nobody worried at all.

For endless complicated and twisted reasons, Katie's dieting became obsessive. By the time she was seventeen and a half (and mind, that's two years later), even Katie's selfish mother took time off from her lovers to worry about her daughter's health.

She used to do quite hopeless but I suppose quite touching things, like leaving doughnuts accidentally on the kitchen table. Well, by this stage Katie was far too interested in herself to waste time feeling touched. She thought her mother was overbearing, and that she was jealous of Katie's youth and her will-power.

As her parents were more worried, Katie found she had to tell more lies. Her timetable was entirely designed to avoid meal times. She joined the school choir, which finished at seven so she could tell her parents she'd eaten at school. Then she'd arrange to meet friends in the evenings. She told her friends she'd eaten at home and she told her parents she was eating with friends. In the mornings she used to get up extra early to give herself time to dirty a cereal bowl and put some breadcrumbs on a plate before the others came down.

And of course she became a vegetarian.

Then a vegan.

And she lost more and more weight.

Nobody could understand it. After all she used to give such incredibly detailed descriptions of the delicious cheesecake she'd eaten last night. But nobody ever actually *saw* her eat the delicious cheesecakes, or the lasagne, or the Big Macs. She never slipped up. Her lies were beautiful. They were perfectly worked out, and after all so they should be. Katie was an intelligent girl, and every ounce of her brain power was put towards deceiving all the lunatics around her who seemed to want to force her back into obesity.

So things got worse and worse. Katie was by now very, very thin and her character had changed. She was deceitful and shifty and irritable and lifeless. She lost a lot of friends and every single one of her admirers.

On one Friday evening Katie's father lost his temper and told his daughter that she was repulsive to look at. Why couldn't she just behave like normal people and have a healthy appetite? He said she couldn't go out on the town until she sat at the table and ate a full plate of spaghetti right there in front of him. So Katie had flown into a rage and left the kitchen sobbing hysterically. She'd been sulking in her bedroom ever since.

By Sunday lunch-time she still hadn't emerged and her parents were not only angry but also quite seriously worried. They decided to have a conversation about their forgotten daughter, which was quite odd in itself.

Mr Dye was firm and wise and manly, and his wife remembered for the first time in ages why she'd ever fallen in love with him. She almost wanted to forget the whole saga of her bloody-minded daughter and just carry right on flirting.

But sensible Mr Dye would hear of no such thing. He wanted to get this whole thing sorted out here and now. He was fed up with beating about the bush.

Mrs Dye agreed.

Katie's father said he was going to fetch the girl down from her bedroom, if necessary by force, and bring her into the kitchen where Mrs Dye was already to have prepared a big hot plate of Sunday lunch leftovers. Katie would be told that unless she ate every single mouthful of it then she must pack her bags and leave. They could really do nothing else for her.

His wife agreed. It may sound too heartless, but Mrs Dye loved drama, and she had very little understanding of what was going on. She stubbed out her cigarette and carried her elegant drink into the kitchen. Oriel, the little boy (heaven knows why they called him that – they'd gone up in the world) followed whining behind.

Mrs Dye waited and listened. She was feeling quite nervous.

Surprisingly soon afterwards she heard her husband close Katie's bedroom door and walk down the stairs towards the kitchen. He was talking calmly and pompously to his eldest child. He, too, was quite clearly enjoying himself.

As I say, the Dyes were bored, they had everything they needed and more. Here was a bit of drama in which they could act out a most important role. Understanding parents with mixed-up, stroppy teenager.

'I'm glad to see you're being a bit more reasonable now, Katie. You shouldn't fly off the handle so easily. Being adult means coping with the little hiccups in life. You can't do everything you want to all the time. And it's not as if we haven't done our best for you. When I was your age I didn't know where the next meal was coming from. You know by now how Granny used to have to take in other people's washing to feed us . . .'

Mr Dye squared his shoulders.

'Well, I'm glad to say that *that's* all been taken care of. Your grandmother certainly doesn't want for anything now . . . So who are you to be turning your spoilt little nose up at good food? Don't you know that half the world is starving? You're a very lucky girl, Katie Dye, and don't you forget it.'

Katie didn't talk. She was too busy thinking about herself and how angry she was. Didn't he realise that she was nearly eighteen? He didn't *own* her any more. She was her own person and she would *not* be made to do anything she didn't want to do. How *dared* he order her out of her bedroom like that?

Oh, but she didn't know what was coming next.

They reached the kitchen, and there on the table was an enormous plateful of luke-warm, dark brown roast beef, at least four potatoes, Yorkshire pudding, carrots, peas, parsnips, cabbage, and all set off with what looked like three tumbler's worth of thick beige-coloured gravy. The plate was piled high, high, high and the gravy was dripping off the edges and spilling on to the new mahogany kitchen table. Beside it was a large bowl of Bird's Eye trifle. Not even a hard-working farmer could have found it appetising, and it seems to me that there might have been an element of sadism going on from the glint in Mrs Dye's beautifully made-up eyes.

Mr Dye was quite taken aback by the sight of Katie's lunch. But he'd come too far now, and he wasn't a man to alter his decisions. He pushed Katie in the direction of the food and told her to sit down. Katie refused to look at the plate in front of her, but she sat. Her face was white and she was very angry. Her parents didn't seem to notice. They were both marginally surprised that she sat without arguing. Katie looked straight at her mother, stoney-eyed. Her mother blushed and dropped her eyes to the floor.

Satisfied, Katie turned her gaze towards her father and waited. But he wasn't to be put off so easily, he just thought his daughter was rather cross.

'It's no good you looking at me like that, Katie, with all your bloody public school airs.'

Katie went on looking at her father and she said nothing.

'Katie, your mother and I have had enough. You don't eat, you look disgusting, you lose your temper when either of us even suggest you stay in one evening and eat with us. What's got into you? You used to be such a sunny little girl. We've always done our best for you, you've never wanted for anything have you, and what bloody thanks do we get? A sulky, selfish piece of stick who can't address a civil word to the people who've devoted their whole bloody lives to you.

'Now as I say, we've had enough. And we're going to give you just one more chance, is that clear?'

Katie just watched him. She didn't reply.

'Is that clear?'

Somehow Mr Dye knew he wouldn't get an answer and he decided not to make an issue of it. He was coming up to the important bit, and he didn't want to be lead astray.

'Unless you eat every single mouthful of food on these two plates, you can get out. We can't do anything more for you. Do you understand? You can get out. You can pack your bags and get out of the house. Just go and see how well you survive on your own two feet. You wouldn't even get past the end of the bloody drive!'

Katie still didn't say anything. She'd never been threatened like this before, but it didn't occur to her to take it seriously. She had absolutely no intention of eating their leftovers. For the first time she looked at the plate in front of her. She felt her stomach turn.

'You've forgotten, I'm a vegetarian,' Katie said it with an icy calm.

'Balls you're a vegetarian, you just never fucking eat!'

Katie was alarmed, she'd never heard her father speak like that before. For the first time she began to take his threats more seriously.

Mrs Dye said, 'Brian, don't be too hard on the girl.'

'And you can shut up, you're no bloody help are you? Some bloody mother you've been to the girl, waltzing around the country with a different man on your arm every week!'

So he *did* know. Mrs Dye looked terrified and she shut up. He turned back to the girl.

'Well? Are you going to eat it or aren't you? I'll give you ten seconds and if you haven't picked up that knife and fork by then, I'm sending your mother to your room to pack. DO YOU UNDERSTAND?'

Katie looked from her father to the food and back again. She wasn't afraid. But she was angry. She felt the room spin with her suppressed anger and then her father crossed his arms and leant against a kitchen unit opposite.

'One . . .'

Katie hadn't eaten for a long time, but when she heard her father's complacent 'one' she thought she was going to be sick.

'two . . .'

Katie felt her eyes smarting, and then she suddenly felt the irresistible urge to laugh.

'three . . .'

Katie's shoulders began to shake. Her face was quite expressionless, but her eyes were still smarting.

'four . . .'

Katie felt a tear roll down her left cheek, and she heard a hollow laugh echoing from the depths of her empty stomach.

'five . . .'

Her heart was beating fast, and slowly, very slowly she could feel her arms lifting themselves from her lap. They reached for the knife and fork.

Her father was silent, he was watching her.

Katie's hands rested on top of the knife and fork on either side of the plate. She was quite still.

Her father waited. 'Pick them up, Katie.'

She didn't.

'PICK THEM UP.'

No.

'six . . .'

Then Katie's laughter became more audible. She picked up the knife and fork, she stared at them. She heard her father telling her to eat and quite suddenly, still laughing – even louder now, she dropped them and with both hands she grabbed the four potatoes lying cold on her plate. Her hands were covered in the gravy. She looked up at her father and she watched him as he watched her stuffing them into her mouth. She smeared the potato and the gravy all over her face and she reached for the beef, not taking her eyes off her father all the while. Potato was spilling out of her mouth, but she crammed it all back in again and somehow made space for the beef. And she kept on and on laughing. She made another grab for her plate and she scraped up all that remained. She held it in front of her and she kept on chewing, kept on laughing.

Her mother and father stood at far sides of the kitchen, frozen, mesmerised.

The gravy and the beef and the potato were all over her face, and more was falling out of her mouth all the time. She still watched her father and she raised her cupped hands to her face again. She pushed it all in and she rubbed the remainder all over her face. She reached for the trifle and she kept on chewing. She took one gravied, bloodied hand and very carefully scooped out the bowl's entire contents. She watched it dribble through her fingers, still chewing, still laughing, and she clenched her fist. She watched it all slop down on to the mahogany table. The she dipped her head and buried her face in its mess.

Her shoulders were still shaking when she looked up to enjoy her father's expression. They stared at each other and quite suddenly Katie stopped laughing. Her tears were mingling with the trifle and the gravy.

Her father took a step forward. But Katie raised her hand. She stood up.

'No, wait, I haven't finished yet.' Then she started to laugh once again. Very carefully, Katie rolled up her sleeves. She pushed her hair away from her face and she leant forward, right over the kitchen table, always looking at her father.

He watched.

She lifted her hand to her mouth and she stuck two fingers down her throat. She retched twice and her mother screamed.

Then she vomited, and all the food that could barely even have got to her stomach poured right out all over the mahogany table. She vomited three times and then there was nothing left.

Her parents stood there and Katie looked down at her vomit. She was no longer angry, she was appalled. She collapsed back into the chair and threw her whole weight on to the table, back into her vomit, and she sobbed.

Her father didn't move. For a few seconds he just watched her. Then, very quietly, he said:

'Get out.'

Katie stayed where she was.

'Did you hear me? Get out!'

She didn't look up. 'Oh, my God ... I'm sorry, Dad, please, I'm sorry ...'

'It's too late now, Katie, you've gone too far now.' He turned to his wife. 'Go and collect her stuff, she's getting out.'

Mrs Dye was crying, all she said was, 'Brian.'

He turned towards her as if he were about to hit her. 'Get her stuff, woman, she's leaving.'

She cowered and edged out of the room.

Soon afterwards he couldn't bear to be left alone with his daughter any more. He turned and went up the stairs. Katie heard him shouting and what seemed like only a second later he returned, his wife tripping hopelessly behind. He threw a suitcase in his daughter's direction, and he threw her her car keys.

'Now, go. And don't you ever dare to come back. You're no good to us, you're no daughter of mine.'

Katie couldn't move. She stayed with her face in her vomit and she pleaded. He lunged towards her, picked up the suitcase in one hand and his daughter by the scruff of her neck with the other, and threw them both out of the front door.

Katie lay in the heap where she landed and cried quite hysterically for a while. At first she thought her parents might take pity, but soon she realised that the door would never be opened for her again. When she understood that, a certain amount of energy came back to her. She'd make them pay for what they'd done. One day they'd be grovelling outside *her* front door. She picked herself up and carried the suitcase to the car. She felt quite strong now, but it won't last. She only really feels so strong because she's angry.

As she drove towards London, which, as she lived in Berkshire, wasn't too far away, Katie worked out what she was going to do with the rest of her life. Most importantly she wanted to be a success. She wanted her parents to curse themselves for throwing her away. Maybe she should be a television presenter, after all she was perfectly pretty enough, and she knew she had a pleasantly educated-sounding voice, her father was always telling her so. Or maybe she should just marry a lord. *Then* her parents would come crawling back. Katie laughed aloud. That brought her back to the present. She thought, but what am I going to do *tonight*, I haven't got a penny?

Well, she stayed in a bed and breakfast on the Shepherd's Bush Road. She'd never stayed anywhere so horrible in her life before. It came as quite a shock. The next day she took her car to a rather seedy-looking garage and said she needed a quick sale, for cash. Poor Katie was completely ripped off, and worse still, she knew it. Her beautiful six-month-old Mini

Metro only fetched five hundred pounds in grubby ten-pound notes. Still, that should keep her head above water until she found a job and a cheaper place to live.

After two weeks, Katie's anger had subsided, and she was lonely and broke and miserable and out of work. She thought maybe the whole incident at home had blown quite out of proportion. She decided to ring home, and it took a lot of nerve.

She dialled the number and Mr Dye answered. Katie could barely support herself with fear. Her mouth was dry but eventually she managed to get it out.

'Hello, Dad? . . . It's me . . . Katie.'

There was a long pause, and then the telephone went dead. He'd hung up.

So at last Katie accepted that she really was alone in this world. He'd left her the car and now she could do what she wanted.

Her two months alone in London were probably the most miserable of Katie's life. She made no friends, and she found that she was quite incapable of holding a job down for more than a week. And they weren't very taxing jobs either, just waitressing ones in various cheap little restaurants around west London. Katie had been spoilt. For the first time she couldn't do and have whatever she wanted immediately that it occurred to her.

Katie ate a little more than she used to at home. Maybe it was because of the shock, maybe it was because nobody really gave a damn whether she ate or not any more, maybe it was because for the first time in her silly life she realised her own life was her own struggle, and if she wanted to die then nobody could really do much to stop her. Maybe for the first time she realised she had a lot to live for.

She saw the advertisement for 'assistant manageress, no experience required' at the Old Rectory Family Hotel, at a point when things were more than usually desperate. She

93

hadn't been able to find herself a job for three weeks and she'd spent every single penny she could lay her hands on. She already owed her hostel one week's rent, and by tomorrow that would be two.

She didn't know where her next meal was coming from, and that was quite intolerable. Suddenly she felt very indignant and very hungry. She wrote the letter to the hotel immediately. It sounded ideal. She'd be surrounded by a family again, she wouldn't have to worry about her next meal or her next bed, and she'd be doing a respectable job that could even be said to be leading somewhere. Katie knew there was a lot of money in the catering and hotel businesses, and all her romantic illusions about poverty had crumbled to the floor. Katie was sure – she was determined – that she'd be rich again.

Katie somehow managed to borrow the money to get to Shrewsbury from a fellow guest at the hostel, and the rest you know.

So there you have it. Not a pretty tale.

CHAPTER 7

WHILE CHRISTINE WAS enjoying herself interviewing the seven bright sparks back at the Rectory, Rufus had been doing some thinking. He was alone in the flat and the daily telephone calls from his loved ones weren't really making the hours – days – tick by any faster.

He had to admit it, he was bored with his book. And for once in his life he made a decision without discussing it with anyone else first. It was time he found himself a serious job. He would shelve his book until another day. Rufus didn't want to move entirely away from the arts, although he knew that the real money was somewhere else.

On his usual social round of influential smarty-arty friends, he dropped a lot of heavy hints by politely asking their opinion about what he should be doing. One evening he met up with the Australian millionaire again, and at the time he was quite surprisingly sober. So sober, in fact, that he spent the whole evening trying not to catch the millionaire's eye. Every time he thought about the last time they'd met, Rufus felt a flood of redness pour into his cheeks.

Rufus and the millionaire were at the time at what can only be described as a 'supper party'. There were, I suppose, about thirty people eating from a buffet in the house of an up-and-coming young novelist who'd just had a book come out.

Both Rufus and the millionaire, if only they knew it, had one big thing in common that night. They were the only two in the room who hadn't troubled to buy, read or even glimpse at their host's new book.

Rufus should have known better, but he could afford to be sloppy. He was a regular feature on the scene. But the Australian, whom everyone was *mad* for at the moment, had a lot to learn. They'd soon grow tired of his refreshing vulgarity and he would be expected to keep abreast with things like the rest of them. Rufus's friends flattered themselves that there were plenty of Australian millionaires who dug their arty scene. Actually, I doubt it very much, but that makes little – or no – difference.

Anyway, the poor Australian, whose name, by the way, is Arthur Bonneval, was trying to avoid the novelist because he realised he'd made a bit of a *faux pas*, and because he was so new on the scene, he really knew very few other people in the room. So he and his girlfriend found themselves rather lonely. The girlfriend wasn't too worried. She took life as it came. In fact she'd spotted Rufus much earlier in the evening and she'd refrained from mentioning it to her partner. She knew he loved a familiar face, but she could only think, from what the Voguette had told her, that Rufus was a weirdo, however smart, and best kept away from. Right now the beautiful girlfriend was standing with her back to the room, facing the Australian millionaire, who was pretending to listen to her conversation but in fact looking over her shoulder and feeling rather pleased with himself because he'd at last seen someone on whom he could practise his newly acquired smooth greeting.

96

In the middle of his girlfriend's – probably not very interesting – sentence (but still), he said, 'Excuse me,' and pushed her aside by the shoulder. She must have noticed, but she didn't seem to mind.

The Australian walked with some purpose right into the middle of the room. He wanted everyone to watch.

He was just about to grab Rufus by the top of his arm and exclaim great pleasure at bumping into him again, when he realised he couldn't remember the bloody man's name. He stopped quite suddenly just a foot away from his target. Rufus had seen him coming, and he could feel the blood crawling back up to his cheeks. When the Australian stopped so abruptly like that, poor Rufus imagined the worst.

Of course he'd recognised Rufus, but until then he'd entirely forgotten how terribly badly Rufus had behaved. He glanced very quickly at the Australian's face, and he saw the look of anger and embarrassment, so very quickly he turned back to the picture restorer opposite and said:

'Yes, it must be lovely to be able to work in Rome, it's something I've always wanted to do.'

The picture restorer was amazed. He wasn't talking about Rome at all. He was telling Rufus about the wealth of treasures he'd rediscovered at Chatsworth during his last visit there only a fortnight ago – on a professional basis of course. In fact he was reminiscing about a pair of incredible Chinese vases that had been in the room where he was working.

So the picture restorer tried to catch up. He thought he must have missed out on something along the line.

'Yes, it's a fantastic city. You'd think, as a picture restorer, that there'd be plenty of work out there for me. It's an odd thing, but I always seemed to end up in Florence.'

And then they both caught up, so they talked for a while about whether Rome or Florence was the more beautiful – no, surprising – location for a film. Meanwhile, the millionaire who dithered for only a second in mid-step, had turned

97

around, back in the direction of his girlfriend in order to be reminded of the redhead's name.

And now he was retracing his steps, marching with the same ridiculous self-important determination and rehearsing his lines of greeting to the man he'd barely spoken to and had only met once before in his life.

'Rufus!' he said. And he clasped the top of poor Rufus's arm.

Rufus jumped. He was quite getting into the problems of film sets. Then he saw the Australian and all the years of practised ease went right out of the window. He blushed. Then he said, 'Oh heavens,' which was very disappointing.

'Rufus,' said the Australian again, and he tightened his hold on Rufus's arm. Poor man, by now several people were watching and vaguely wondering what would happen next. But the Australian had forgotten his lines. It was up to Rufus again. And he didn't manage particularly well.

'Gosh,' he said, 'what on earth are you doing here?' But it came out far too direct. It sounded almost offensive.

The Australian's awkward, expectant face sort of collapsed.

'I mean, oh dear, that came out awfully, how lovely to see you again so soon.'

The Australian relaxed. 'I don't see your lovely girlfriend here tonight. I hope she's not sick?'

And so Rufus explained that his lovely girlfriend was at home in the country. And then he explained what his lovely girlfriend was doing in the country, and then he explained why she was doing what she was in the country. Maybe Australian millionaires have a way with such things, but by the end of half an hour, Rufus had told him just about everything. And the Australian seemed to be genuinely interested and genuinely concerned.

'I can see that you've suffered a great deal in the past few months.'

Rufus was slightly embarrassed by that, so he mumbled something about his mother feeling it worse. Then he said:

'I think perhaps I owe you and your girlfriend an apology. I don't think I was on my best form the last time we met.'

The millionaire thumped his companion on the back and said, 'Don't you give it another moment's thought.'

But Rufus was being silly and emotional again. He'd decided that he sincerely liked the Australian, and he wanted to put the record straight. So for the first time since it happened, Rufus explained what really happened that night between him and the Voguette.

The Australian listened hard. He was a nice man, but he didn't really understand the significance of what Rufus was telling him. But then I don't suppose he was heavily tuned into either anorexia or drug addiction. *He* was a mover and a shaker, as they say Down Under. Anyway, he listened, and he tried to sympathise, which is all that matters really, and Rufus felt strangely comforted. At the end of it all the Australian just thumped his friend on the back again and repeated what he said before:

'Don't you give it another moment's thought.'

They both laughed, and for a moment they were at a loss as to what to say next. The looked awkwardly into their empty glasses.

'Can I get you a refill?' said Rufus.

Bonneval looked across at the stacks of cheap white wine on the drinks table. He pursed his lips rather uncharacteristically, and then he grinned.

'It's pretty vile, isn't it? Why don't we move on to some place else?'

Rufus looked anxiously in the direction of the beautiful girlfriend, but Arthur said impatiently, 'Oh forget her, she's enjoying herself. Let's go to my club and get arseholed.'

Oh.

Rufus thought it sounded like a wonderful idea, so the two

99

of them skulked out of the room without a farewell to anyone.

They laughed a lot once they got into the taxi, but then Rufus said:

'What about your girlfriend? Will she be able to get home all right?'

And the Australian waved it aside. 'Forget it, man,' he said. 'You and me are going to have fun tonight. We don't want any bloody women dragging behind us *ce soir*.' He chuckled, he was pleased with the French, and so, for some reason, was Rufus. They both said *ce soir* again and the Australian kissed his hand. Like schoolchildren, they both collapsed into giggles. Rufus felt happier at that moment than he had done for a long, long time. And I'll tell you, the Australian may have had a happier temperament anyway, and both of them were by now pretty drunk, but he was in the same over-excited – elated – mood as his companion.

Anyway, eventually they arrived at some obviously incredibly expensive but totally unheard of club, *près de* Harrods, and the Australiàn, who was already a member, absolutely swore by it.

'There are always some pretty hot chicks here, you know, but tonight I just feel like a man-to-man talk and a lot of booze.'

Rufus was half disappointed, half relieved to hear it. None of his other male friends ever took him to kitsch places like this. It was tremendously funny, and he wouldn't have admitted it, but it was also tremendously exciting. He was supposed to be a serious member of society, and serious members of any liberal societies don't fritter their evenings with Australian millionaires in questionable clubs *près de* Harrods. In a sober moment he prayed he wouldn't meet anyone he knew. And you can never be too sure about the hostesses. The most respectable girls are sometimes driven to it. Maybe he'd bump into a god-daughter dressed in camisole knickers and fishnet tights. Now *that* wouldn't be funny for either of them.

They were led to a table, and the Australian, true to form, ordered a magnum of some incredibly grand vintage champagne. Rufus tried to be ashamed and he tried not to be impressed.

'So tell me, Rufus, what do you do with your day? It's about the only thing you haven't explained.' He laughed and Rufus roared, but he didn't like the question.

'Well, until last week I was half-way through writing this bloody book about some artist that nobody's ever heard of and nobody will ever be interested in. Then suddenly I realised that the bloody man bored me pretty rigid too, so I've shelved it.'

The Australian poured some more champagne, and as he did so he said, 'Oh Gawd,' in a specially pronounced English accent. There was no particular reason for him to have said it, you can see that for yourself, and it certainly wasn't fantastically funny, but that one killed them. The tears were falling down their cheeks and their sides were aching and still they couldn't stop laughing. Rufus was the first to straighten up, wipe his eyes and breath out, 'Oh dear.'

There was a pause. Then the Australian guffawed and said 'Oh Gawd' again so that put a stop to any further conversation for another ten minutes. Then quite suddenly the Australian was serious.

'So come on then, man, what are you going to do with the next fifty years of your life?'

Rufus's smile faded. 'To be absolutely honest with you, I really haven't got a clue. I want to get out of London. I want a job that takes me out of my bloody flat.'

'Jesus, Rufus, you sound like my ex-wife.'

'Oh Gawd!' So they were off again.

Several glasses of champagne later the Australian was quite worried about the young man sitting opposite him. He was probably fifteen or twenty years Rufus's senior, and he felt quite paternal towards his drinking companion. Suddenly he said:

'But of course! I've got just the job for you.'

Rufus had been talking about what a pillar of strength Christine had been throughout the whole nasty business and how he didn't know what he'd do without her, so he was rather surprised by Arthur's outburst.

'Listen, Rufus,' he said, 'I've got companies all over the world. You name the country, I'll have a company there.'

'Andorra?'

For a moment the Australian looked as though he might be going to be annoyed, but then his face cracked and he leant back on his chair and roared. 'No, I've got to admit, there's no part of me in Andorra, I'll have to get working on that.'

So they giggled hopelessly for a while. Then the Australian picked up where he left off.

'You've probably learnt somewhere along the line that the good employers wind up the rich ones,' said Arthur.

Rufus remembered something he'd been told by useful Christine about the hair salons provided for staff at Marks and Spencers. He supposed whoever owned that must be pretty damn rich, so he nodded wisely.

'Now, you're an attractive, personable man, aren't you? You've a great deal of charm, OK?'

Rufus couldn't think, in his hazy drunken state, where this might be leading, and true to his English form, he felt incredibly embarrassed. He tried the 'Oh Gawd' trick again, but somehow it didn't seem to work. Neither of them laughed.

'I need a man with charm and personality to be my companies' morale booster. It may sound a bit far-fetched, call it what you will, but I'm prepared to offer you a three-month trial contract to travel around the world, expenses paid of course, and give talks to the workers at each of my plants.

You can talk about whatever you want, I suppose art's your thing, but as long as you remember that your basic function is to cheer up my men and make them think they're lucky to be working for Bonneval and Co., then you've done your job. What do you say?'

Rufus looked doubtful. He wasn't used to making decisions without Christine close at hand.

'What, so I'd be sort of Bonneval and Co.'s chief morale booster?'

'That's right, so what do you say?'

'And I could talk about any subject under the sun, just as long as they went away with your love in their hearts?'

'That's right. Come on, man, it's not as if you've got anything particular lined up for the next three months anyway, have you? What have you got to lose? At the worst it's a three-month freebie travel around the world. You said yourself you wanted to get out of London. What are you waiting for?'

'I think I ought to discuss it first with my lovely girl-friend . . .'

'For God's sake, man, just for once stand on your own two feet. She can't change your bloody nappies for ever. It's time you were able to make a decision for yourself. What do you say?'

Rufus thumped his empty champagne glass back on to the table, and he swayed slightly as he did it.

'By God, you're absolutely right!' he bellowed, and Arthur, who was taken quite by surprise, jerked backwards and slumped on to his chair. With some difficulty he pushed himself forward again. For a moment it looked as though he would collapse back on to the table, but he caught his head with his hands just in time and rested his elbows on the table.

'So what do you say?' he said again.

'I say you're absolutely on. It sounds like a fantastic idea. When do I start?'

Arthur looked pleased. But having won his battle he refused to discuss details out of the office. He'd ring Rufus first thing in the morning, and they'd make arrangements from there.

Several hours later, and many too many drinks, the two men heaved back out into the streets. They seemed to think that they'd formed a lifelong friendship. Rufus knew about all of Arthur's three ex-wives, and he knew how the millionaire had started off at the tender age of seventeen cleaning shoes at Sydney airport. And Arthur knew that Rufus needed a bit of a kick to get him going, that he was a very unhappy man, and that too much had been done for him all his life. Arthur, the good man, intended to change all that.

Well, outside the club Rufus and Arthur hugged each other warmly, and Arthur swore he'd ring up first thing in the morning to arrange a business lunch. They caught separate taxis home. And they both took their rides with the feeling that they'd achieved something that evening. Apart from anything else, they both knew they'd found themselves a soul mate and lifelong friend. That was great.

The next morning Rufus woke much earlier than he usually did. His heart was beating fast and for a while he couldn't think why. Then he thought it was because of his hangover. Poor Rufus's stomach was churning something rotten and he had a seriously unpleasant taste on the roof of his mouth. But we all know what a hangover feels like, no need to waste any more precious words describing *that*. It was half-past seven and Rufus looked across at the telephone. Well, he couldn't expect his friend to ring before nine. Maybe he wouldn't ring at all. Maybe it had been just another drunken conversation. Maybe Rufus had just dreamt it all. Now that *did* give him a fright. But then he felt the top of his mouth and the churning in his stomach. No, it was all very real.

Rufus crawled out of bed and did all the things that people do when they're feeling rotten and they know it's their own fault. He was still in his pyjamas and just taking his first sip of coffee when the telephone rang. Rufus put down his coffee cup and leaped towards the telephone. Then he wished he hadn't. He clutched his stomach and counted to three. He picked up the receiver and said 'Hello' in a sensible voice. After all, it was still only eight o'clock. Even his wonderful Australian should know better than to ring people so early in the morning. Arthur's healthy voice boomed into Rufus's ear.

'Good morning, old man, how are you feeling today?'

If it had been anyone else, Rufus would have groaned and said 'Ghastly', but to his new best friend, he thought it'd probably be better to pretend.

'Fine, fine, fine, never felt better.'

Anyway, the Australian said it was better to get things moving immediately and poor Rufus thought he'd heard that somewhere before. They arranged to meet for lunch in four hours' time and Rufus wondered whether he ought to wear a suit. He didn't. It wasn't his style and he felt sure that it wasn't Arthur's either.

They ate lunch at the Caprice and Bonneval put down his golden American Express card to pay for it at the end of the meal. Rufus wondered if that wasn't a little unnecessary. He wondered if the kind Australian wasn't perhaps showing off a bit there. But he didn't comment.

Anyway, all arrangements were settled. Rufus was to fly on the following Monday, and he wasn't to return for the next three months. He was being paid the most ridiculously large amount just to cheer people up. And his expenses allowance was enough to make a sane person reel. Arthur was proving to be much more than just a lively drinking companion.

As sane Rufus did indeed reel out on to Arlington Street, it suddenly occurred to him that perhaps his lovely girlfriend wouldn't be quite so delighted by the news. Rufus couldn't exactly work out why, but he was sure that he definitely wasn't looking forward to telling her about it.

Today was Tuesday – that left him six days. Why did everything in his life always have to be so sudden? Still, it was better than being bored. He thought about catching a train straight up to Shropshire without even returning to the flat. But he remembered the last unannounced arrival back home, and although he knew that nothing could possibly be up with Christine in charge, he still felt unwilling to risk it.

So he went home and thought about the future. Rufus had an art degree, and the Australian had asked to see his portfolio. Rufus prayed that Christine would remember where he'd put it. Arthur had said that if he liked the work, and if Rufus proved to be as valuable an employee as it seemed he might, then after the three months perhaps Rufus could be put in charge of the artistic side of the companies. That was a big job, and the salary that was suggested was even bigger. Arthur was his fairy godmother. What on earth could he do to repay such kindness? Rufus rang Christine.

'I've got some absolutely brilliant news, but I can't tell you what it is over the telephone.'

Christine said, 'Don't be silly, Rufus, there's nothing that can't be said over the phone,' but still he refused.

He changed the conversation and asked how the interviews had gone. Did she find someone good? Christine was purposefully vague. She said the new girl should be arriving in six days and after that she was all his. She would be coming up to London probably on Sunday night, and she had to admit, she was looking forward to it.

Rufus felt a sinking feeling in his heart. How was he ever going to tell her that from Monday he was anybody's but hers?

'Christine . . .' Rufus said, 'I've got a job.'

'But Rufus, that's wonderful news. What about your book? Tell me all about it.'

'Well, that's the problem, I mean I'd decided to shelve the book before this job came up . . .'

'Yes, carry on.' Christine already smelt a rat.

Anyway, Rufus eventually got it out — after a lot of humming and hawing and reminding Christine about the Australian they'd both met at Lesley's house not long ago.

Christine was furious. And I suppose in a way she had a right to be. She'd spent the last God knew how long rotting away in the country, she'd lost her job to look after Rufus's crippled family and what thanks did she get? Of course she was pleased that Rufus was so pleased, but what was she supposed to do while he jet-setted off around the world *cheering people up?* 'Honestly, Rufus,' she said, 'when you told me you'd found a job I hoped it might be a little less half baked and frivolous and dead end than *that.*'

Rufus was hurt. He knew Christine wouldn't be pleased about his going off for three months without her, but he'd hoped she'd be quite impressed by the actual job, especially as it promised to lead to still greater things. But Christine didn't accept that. She said she knew about millionaires, and that Rufus was just being made to do other people's dirty work with a promise of a prize at the end of it. It would all come to nothing except three perfectly wasted months. That she was sure of.

'In the meantime,' she said, 'what are we going to do about each other? If you're leaving the country in six days, then I suggest you come up to the Rectory for a couple of days and bid not only me, but your poor, lonely mother a fond farewell.'

'But Christine, you know I can't, I've got to organise my life. I've got to pack and things.'

'Nonsense. It doesn't take six days to put a pair of pyjamas into a suitcase. I can't possibly leave your mother alone down here, that's obvious. So either you come down this week or I suppose we just don't see each other for another three months. If that's what you want . . . well . . . what can I say?'

Rufus sighed. He had no choice, and to be honest I think

he was being quite selfish trying to get out of going home anyway. So he said OK, and he told Christine which train he'd be on in the morning. They said goodbye to each other rather grumpily. They both thought the other was being quite intolerable. And to a certain extent, they were both right.

Christine met Rufus at Shrewsbury station the next morning and the two of them greeted one another sulkily. They'd both been brooding about the other's unreasonableness all night, and they'd whipped themselves up into quite a fury. Christine drove, and for the first two miles of the six-mile journey, she drove in silence. Then Rufus began to feel rather uncomfortable so he started three conversations. One about the train journey, one about the fascist taxi driver who'd brought him to the station, and the last about the progress of the new hotel. Christine just answered in sensitive monosyllables, so eventually he gave up.

They drove in silence again for another two miles. Then Christine spoke. She said:

'Rufus, it's no good, you can't just win me round with social small talk. You've hurt me very badly, and it's an insult to my intelligence that you think conversation about your bloody taxi driver is going to make up for it.'

Rufus sighed. God, Christine could be hell sometimes.

'Sorry, love,' he said.

'And don't say sorry when you don't mean it.'

'But I am sorry, darling, I really am.' Poor Rufus just wanted a bit of peace. He was otherwise in such a frenzy of over-excitement. Typical Christine to try and dampen his joy.

'But how can I know you mean it, Rufus. How do I know you're not just going to waltz off for another six months without even consulting me first when you've come back from this ridiculous little trip?'

'I promise I won't, love,' he said. 'I'm sorry if you think I've been selfish.' God, he wished, she'd shut up.

'I don't believe you're really sorry, I just don't believe it.'

He didn't say anything. He wanted to punch her in the face but he thought it might be dangerous, and anyway it really wouldn't do much good.

'*Please* be nice, darling. You must see that I have a right to complain.'

And so it went on. At some point, for some lunatic reason of her own, Christine decided to believe Rufus's repeated apologies. She kissed him then and said, 'You *were* a bit selfish, weren't you, darling? It's just men, they can't think outwards like women do. Never mind, we shan't say another word about it.'

Rufus heaved a sigh of relief and prepared to greet his dotty old mother. But when he saw her, he was quite surprised by how un-dotty or old she looked. But I'm afraid it was only skin deep. She'd smartened up her act. Christine had taken her to Marks and Spencers and forced her to buy some respectable clothes. She said, I suppose quite rightly, that professional women couldn't go around in dirty shirts and paint-stained trousers.

So at last Mrs Burton looked like a county lady again. She was wearing a sensible woollen tweed skirt and a pale brown shirt with a bow around the neck. Christine had thought that that was sensible for a woman of Isobel's age. Isobel couldn't have cared less. When it came to clothes, as by now with most things, she let Christine wear the trousers.

Home was cleaner than he'd ever seen it before. But Rufus couldn't get used to other people's cars parked right outside his front door, or the smell of other people's tobacco having as much right in the hall as the smell of his own. There was no privacy left, and although he tried hard to think that the hotel was a good thing, and really he knew it was, he couldn't help dreaming about the old days. Why did his mother have to go and spend so much money anyway? It was too silly, but he started to resent his mother's last twenty-one years of extravagance. Rufus was very restless during his two-day stay at the Rectory. And Christine thought that he seemed to be rather detached. The spell alone in London had spoilt him. He'd grown selfish, she was sure.

Rufus was dying for Monday and he was dying to get away from Christine. It seemed to him she'd devoted her entire energy into picking quarrels from the moment he'd arrived. He'd never thought of her as a jealous person before. But that was it, he was sure.

The truth was, and it's quite obvious, Christine didn't like Rufus's new lease of independence. She'd always taken Rufus's dependence on her for granted and although she often used to complain, she suddenly felt quite insecure without it. She was without a job, and now she worried that she might even be without a role. So Rufus left the Rectory to go back to London in much the same over-excited way that he used to leave as a child when he was going back to prep school. It hurt Christine still more than it used to hurt his mother. Then they could say he was only young.

Rufus met up with his boss only one more time before he left the country, but he had endless conversations with the secretary who'd got everything beautifully organised. First stop – Hong Kong.

So while Rufus was organising his jet-set wardrobe and wondering what the climate would be like in Hong Kong, Christine had been worrying more and more about Katie Dye. She wasn't usually someone who doubted the wisdom of her decisions, but this time she thought she may have made a dreadful mistake. There was one thing she was quite sure about: she wouldn't be there when Katie and Isobel first met.

Now, Christine is no coward, and she reasoned with herself, quite understandably, that she'd done enough for other people for the time being, and from Sunday night she was going to do what *she* wanted to do. And she wanted to see Rufus before he left.

CHAPTER 8

CHRISTINE WAS THE daughter of lapsed Jewish parents who had never taken her to the synagogue and had very seldom gone there themselves. So Christine, who preferred to think about more practical things, didn't really belong to any church at all. During her adolescence she'd dabbled in Buddhism but that was just to be provocative and interesting and nobody had paid much attention. So now she called herself an agnostic.

She was an only child and she'd been sent to a suitably smart and expensive London girls' school where she'd always been popular and always done well in exams. Much to the disappointment of her parents and teachers, Christine had refused to sit for Oxford, she kept mumbling something about elitism – she disapproved – so she went to Sussex instead. She read history, smoked a lot of dope, went to a lot of parties, had a wonderful time, and came away with an upper second. Everyone was delighted.

When she was twenty-four her rich parents were both killed in an avalanche on the Alps during their annual two-week skiing trip. Christine was very brave and her friends and Jewish relations, who'd always rather disapproved of Christine's parents, all flocked round and were a tremendous support. So at twenty-four Christine was a rich and highly eligible young maiden with a lot of respectable left-wing ideas.

When she was twenty-nine she met Rufus. She'd had a lot of half-hearted affairs in the five years since her parents had died. But she was lonely and she always used to frighten her suitors off by her overbearing desperation.

Her life took a turn for the better when she met Rufus. He was warm and generous, with a family, and he depended on her. Just what Christine needed. She had to give something in return for the family, and she was the strong, supportive – maternal – type.

So you can see that Christine needed Rufus really as much as Rufus needed her. And they mixed in the same set, which always makes things easier.

★   ★   ★

Christine took the train to London on Sunday night, and left Isobel alone (apart from the guests) for the first time, I think, since Rufus's traumatic discovery. But she would only be alone for a night. Christine had seen to it that there was supper in the fridge and a good video in the machine in case she still didn't feel like painting.

She *did* feel a bit guilty as she watched Isobel waving her off, alone and trying hard to look cheerful, on Shrewsbury station. Still, she wasn't going to see Rufus for another three months, and Isobel had to be left alone at some point. She really couldn't be expected to look after her until she died.

Rufus was feeling rotten, as well he might, about his behaviour at the Rectory. He'd spoken to Christine several times since then, and relations were much better. He was looking forward to seeing her again.

They met at the station and it was rather touching, they sort of fell into each other's arms. For the first time, Rufus began to have second thoughts about the three months' separation. If only Christine could come with him. Like a wise man, he communicated his wish, and Christine was delighted. But then she realised it was the first time he's said so which rather dampened her joy.

They decided as it was their last night together for some time, that they would be extravagant, which they generally were anyway, so they took a taxi to Soho and ate dinner in the Red Fort. Then they stumbled home fairly merry and made a lot of passionate love. They hadn't been together for a long time.

Rufus wasn't due to leave London until lunch-time, and Christine, with her new, jobless freedom, said she would accompany him to the airport. Neither admitted it, but they were both feeling pretty nervous. This would be their longest separation since the day they first met.

After a deal of fussing, Rufus and Christine eventually went their separate ways. He promised to telephone her as soon as he reached his hotel in Hong Kong – Christine was one of those people who are terrified of flying – and Christine caught the tube back home. She was depressed. She had no idea what she was going to do once she got back to the flat. Christine wouldn't look for a job today, she couldn't possibly just do it in cold blood. First she must get back into circulation. That was by far the most effective method of job hunting.

Back in the flat Christine lit a cigarette and wondered who to call. Now it came to the crunch, she didn't really want to talk to anybody. She thought of ringing Isobel but then she decided to wait a couple of days, let her and Katie both get into the swing of things.

She puffed up a cushion in the drawing room and looked

at her watch. It was still too early for a drink. She lit another cigarette. There was something the matter with her, she wasn't usually so lethargic.

The telephone rang. Her problems were solved, she would find out all the gossip and try to arrange something with whoever it was on the line. She certainly didn't want to spend the evening alone.

It was the Australian, he was ringing to check that Rufus had gone off all right.

'But I won't keep you, lovely,' he said, 'I'm sure you're too busy enjoying your first few days of freedom to be wanting to talk to me. I'll leave you to it and I'm sure we'll meet up soon.'

He was gone.

And it was still too early to get herself a drink. The trouble was, all her friends were in their offices right now, they'd be far too busy to want to talk to her, and perhaps they wouldn't want to see her anyway, now that Rufus was away. Perhaps all her friends only bore her for Rufus. And it's famous what a trial one half of a partnership is when the other half's gone away. And she was out of a job and she'd been in the country for ages, she wouldn't have anything to say.

Oh dear, poor Christine really *is* in a bad way.

But she didn't want to be out when Rufus eventually rang, and he would probably ring in the middle of the night. She decided to go out and buy a Jackie Collins – something which on the whole she disapproved of most heartily. Yes, she'd stay in tonight, tomorrow she'd get things moving again.

Rufus didn't ring until nine o'clock the next morning. Christine was sure he hadn't rung the moment he arrived, but she didn't want an argument when he was so far away, so she just sounded pleased to hear from him.

It was Rufus who said 'I've got to go, there's a client waiting to see me,' this time, and Christine hung up feeling very bitter. How dared he have important clients to see when she'd sacrificed everything, *everything* for his family – or what there was left of it. What was she expected to do with herself now? She hadn't even got a job any more. She decided she'd already done too much hanging around. It was time to get moving. She made herself a cup of coffee and flicked through her address book.

She would ring every single interior designer or contact she could get hold of. She was good, she kept reminding herself, and the more she reminded herself the less she was convinced. Damn her firm for not being a little more understanding. Damn Rufus for waltzing off into the distance without a care in the world. Damn Christine for being so high-handed and giving in her notice like that. It was unlike her to act out of temper and pride. She was usually so calm and practical. Maybe she needed a break. Yes, she needed a holiday, but this wasn't the time to be worrying about it. First she must find herself a job. So she lit a cigarette, but it was too early in the morning and it made her feel sick. She stubbed it out and started to dial the first number in the list of her contacts. This should be the most hopeful, after all the girl had been a friend – and really quite a good one – for nearly fifteen years. Well, maybe a bit less, they'd been to university together.

But word gets around quickly, and when the woman in question heard Christine's voice on the other end of the telephone, her heart sank. She knew Christine would be looking for a job, and although she quite liked Christine, the idea of working with her, however good she may be, was quite intolerable. The woman had to think quickly.

'Christine! How wonderful to hear from you. I hear your stinking firm gave you the push – or rather the other way around. It'd be so wonderful if you could work with us, but I already looked into it, and we're absolutely fully staffed. But you probably wouldn't want to work with grotty old us anyway. Far too grand for *us*!' She laughed a bit nervously. On quick reflection, that last speech hadn't been delivered with the utmost tact. She shouldn't have rushed it. She curled up her toes in embarrassment while she waited for her great friend's reply.

Christine was taken aback. It hadn't occurred to her that people would already know about the job.

'God! News certainly does travel fast. And I certainly was *not* sacked. Anyway, I just rang up for a chat, we haven't seen each other for ages. Why do people always assume the worst . . .' Christine was at a loss as to what to say next. It was no fun being a beggar and she'd grown spoilt in her comfortable job. She'd forgotten what it was like.

'How are you?' she finished lamely.

'Fine, fine . . . really well. Listen, Chris, I've got to go, there's someone waiting to see me and he's been there all morning. Can I ring you back? You're still at the same address? Brilliant, OK, talk to you later, look forward to it, lots of love.'

And she was gone.

Christine put down the telephone and tried another cigarette. It tasted better but she felt as if she'd just been punched in the stomach. The stupid bitch was supposed to be one of her best friends. Well, she didn't need her. She could get by on her own talent. She looked down at the list of contacts and dialled the number of the next most likely employer.

She wondered if, were the roles reversed and her friend had come begging Christine for a job, whether she'd have treated her with the same cold shoulder. Christine decided absolutely not. But I think she may have been kidding herself. Nobody likes being rung up when they know it's only for a favour.

The next most likely employer was a man, and he'd had the hots for Christine for several years. He too had heard that she might be looking for a job, and he'd also heard that Rufus was out of the country for quite some time. He'd been looking forward to Christine's call.

Christine knew that Simon Billingate-Smith (as, I fear, he was called) had had a weakness for her for ages. And on the occasions that they bumped into each other, she'd always flirted with him to keep his interest up. She would have been furious if one day she had heard he was engaged.

So she flirted even more than usual this time. And Simon enjoyed his new feeling of power. He invited Christine out to dinner, and Christine found herself accepting, well, she had nothing else to do that evening, and anyway, she told herself, he was an old friend; she enjoyed his company.

Anyway, Christine hung up feeling much more cheerful. She had something to do after all. She hadn't actually mentioned her lack of employment to Simon yet, and neither had he mentioned it to her. She didn't know he knew. Well, he would've mentioned it if he did.

She wondered what to wear and whether or not to clip back her hair.

Meanwhile Simon chuckled a most unpleasant chuckle to himself and gazed thoughtfully at his very modern telephone. He thought, she can't just ring me when she wants a favour. I'll claim my favours too and then *perhaps* I'll consider finding her a job. But she certainly can't work here.

And Christine planned at what stage of the meal she might broach the problem of employment. She would have to play it carefully. People were so touchy about being asked for favours.

You see, it didn't occur to her that Simon might be planning to spend their evening together rather less innocently. Without really thinking about it, she assumed he knew that she was as good as married to Rufus, and that Simon's was a lost cause. Well, they'd both misinterpreted each other and the situation. And it serves them both right. Neither of them is a quarter as powerful as they'd like to think they are.

Christine ran herself a bath and lit another cigarette. It was high time she got dressed.

Just before she left to meet Simon for dinner, Rufus rang for the second time that day. He seemed to be in very high spirits. Apparently the orientals were incredibly polite to him. Christine said, read servile and don't be so arrogant. She said European men always came back from the orient sexist, racist pigs, and that Rufus wasn't to let it all go to his head.

She laughed and he laughed and she was dead right and he knew it.

Apparently Bangkok was the next stop. Christine said that that sounded just too exciting while she was stuck in London having dinner with the likes of Billingate-Smith, which reminded her she had to go. She was about to be late. They said they loved each other and then they said goodbye quite cheerfully.

She and Billingate-Smith were supposed to have met at the French House in Dean Street, but when Christine arrived, she saw that he was waiting outside.

He kissed her (on the cheek), his greeting, and to Christine's surprise and annoyance he put his arm straight around her waist. But they were old friends and Christine needed a favour. It wasn't quite bad enough for her to push him off.

'I looked inside,'he said, 'and it looks even seedier than I remembered. Let's go somewhere else.'

Christine noticed his city slicker suit and felt his general merchant banker's aura, and thought it was quite a relief he hadn't decided to go right on in. She didn't particularly want to be seen with him.

So this merchant-banker-cum-interior-designer who only suggested the French House because he thought it might make Christine feel ill at ease, intended to make it a most unpleasant evening for his companion. He'd been planning it all afternoon.

'I gather you've lost your job. You must be having a wonderful holiday – or are you job-hunting already?' he said.

For a moment poor Christine was lost for words. She pulled

herself together. 'Yes, I resigned as a matter of fact. I've been opening a hotel in Shropshire, and that, believe you me, is hardly a holiday.'

'So the most promising young designer in London has opted for the catering business, has she? Come on, Christine, I'm not a fool. If you're not looking for a job, then what on earth are you doing spending a whole evening with *me*? Or perhaps you've discovered that I'm rather good company after all ... or perhaps your lovely young man is a little unforthcoming with that precious golden ring? Is *that* why you're here, darling?' His left hand moved clumsily from her waist to her bottom. He patted her bottom, and then, what with one thing and another, he realised he'd gone too far.

Christine stopped quite still. She turned towards Simon and his arm fell limply from her bottom to his side. He could feel himself reddening, but he kept the silly cocky smirk on his face in an attempt to hide it. Damn it! Why couldn't he have kept to the plan? Now, of course, she'd leave. Nobody was that desperate.

Christine looked at him, and, in a more compassionate mood, she might even have felt a little sorry for him. But right now she was far too angry. And she was most dignified. She looked at him for just a little longer, then without saying a word, she turned around and headed back towards the tube. She heard Simon shouting after her.

'I say, Christine, only joking, can't you take a little joke against yourself once in a while? Only a joke.'

But he stood where he was, he didn't follow her, and as he realised that he'd lost her he stopped pleading and started to hurl the most offensive abuse. Christine just carried on walking. Then she saw a free taxi so she hailed it. She gave the cabman her address and that was the end of a highly unsatisfactory evening.

★   ★   ★

The next morning Christine woke up with a rotten smoking hangover. She must have got through nearly two packets last night. Her mouth tasted horrible and it was very mildly painful to breathe. She made herself a cup of coffee, drank it, felt sick, and looked miserably at her useless list of contacts. Who should she try now?

Well, she rang three really good old friends and the first two were only marginally more friendly towards her than the good old friends she'd tried yesterday. Christine was beginning to have serious doubts about the meaning of friendship and her future in interior design. Maybe she ought to try doing something completely different. After all, she wasn't too old yet. She rang the third person at twelve o'clock, which is famously a time when people in offices are at their most irritable, but it was only then that she received her first remotely positive reply. You see, this time she'd learnt her lesson. She decided not to beat about the bush. She said:

'Hello, Barry, it's Christine here, no doubt you already know I've lost my old job, and surprise, surprise, I'm looking for another one. Hotel management really isn't my thing.' And she laughed.

Well, Barry was incredibly warm, but the problem was, he didn't realise how grand a designer Christine had now become. He wasn't a very close friend or very dedicated to his trade. In fact he was the first person she'd spoken to who didn't even know she was out of a job.

He said he only had a job on the shop floor which wasn't as humble as it might sound. Of course, she would go out on location, and knowing Christine, it was highly unlikely she'd stay at that level for long. He said he was sorry (he did at least know she was a bit grander than that), but at the moment that was their only vacancy.

Christine was furious. Didn't he know that for the past two years she'd been running a company on her own? But she kept quiet, her experiences of the past few days had made her perhaps unnecessarily humble. She said, 'That's great, can I keep it open for a while and have a look around?' But she was hoping for something a bit more specialised.

The two of them said goodbye to each other on the friendliest terms, and poor Christine hung up absolutely miserable. She looked at her watch, perhaps Rufus might ring soon. Now what could she do? Perhaps she could try and drag one of her friends out of their office to meet her for lunch, or perhaps she should ring Isobel.

She wandered into the kitchen and lit a cigarette. She spotted last month's *Cosmopolitan* on top of the fridge, and decided that reading it would be a very fruitful way of spending the morning. For a while she blotted out her misery and her loneliness.

At about four, Rufus rang, and Christine realised that she still hadn't bothered to dress.

CHAPTER 9

ON THE MONDAY morning that Katie Dye caught a train from London to Shewsbury, she wasn't feeling too strong at all. The shock of being turned out of her parents' house had made her eat a certain amount more than she was used to and Katie felt miserably enormous. So for the last three days she hadn't swallowed a thing – apart from laxatives – and although she really did fell pretty ill, at least she didn't despise herself any more. In fact she was feeling rather pleased with herself.

When she lay down, which she did quite often because she didn't have a great deal of energy, not only did her hips jut out at an incredibly pleasing sharp angle, but something very curious seemed to happen to her appendix. It swelled up almost to the level of her hips. It was actually quite painful. Katie assumed it was something to do with the air in her empty (shrivelled) stomach. It didn't really worry her. On the contrary she thought it was a good sign. Because it only happened when her stomach was *really* empty and she was *really* thin. Her appendix had stopped swelling for a while after she'd left home. She was glad it had started again.

So Katie took her suitcase and all her worldly possessions, which for the first time in her life were disappointingly few, and caught the train to the north. On the train Katie watched a fat, over-made-up girl opposite her eat her way through a Topic and a Twix and a daintily mixed Bacardi and Coke. Katie's heart, like her appendix, swelled beautifully but this time it was with a sort of smugness and pride and despising. She wanted to buy the fat girl another Twix and more Topics with extra peanuts. She loved watching other people eat. Over the loudspeaker a bored voice kept telling Katie about hot and cold snacks, toasted sandwiches . . . and suddenly she felt very, very hungry. She told herself that she'd regret it afterwards, but she bought a bacon sandwich and ate it in about one and a half mouthfuls, before she gave herself time to change her mind and throw it away. It gave her a stomach ache, but it didn't satisfy her craving for food. Now she just *had* to have some chocolate . . . And so it carried on. Once she'd finished – and by now her stomach was hurting quite badly – Katie cried. She knew she could feel her skinny face sagging with fresh fat, and that the tops of her arms were bulging out of her shirt. She would've sicked it all up, but the last time she'd done that, it had been so excruciatingly painful, and the glands in her neck had stayed stuck up and swollen. She rummaged in her bag for the laxatives, then she thought (which was surprisingly sensible of her) that she couldn't spend the whole of her first day at work on the lavatory. No, she'd just have not to eat for six days to burn it all off.

It may be difficult to sympathise with Katie. You may think she's egocentric and spoilt and inward-looking. But there's not much question about it, she needs help – although the fact that she wasn't sick and that she chose not to take laxatives is a marked sign of improvement. You would never have caught Anna being so weak.

★　　★　　★

Christine refused to describe Katie to Isobel before she left. She didn't admit it, but in fact she didn't dare. Christine told Isobel that the easiest idea was for her to hold a card at Shrewsbury station with Katie's name, and the name of the hotel. Poor Isobel had very little choice in the matter. Christine even made the card. So at the proper time Isobel was to be found standing most awkwardly holding the card in such a way that as few people as possible could see it. She thought the whole thing was rather common and altogether far too flamboyant. You see, she was really quite extraordinarily old-fashioned and snobbish. She didn't want to be so publicly associated with enterprise, and anyway, she felt like a holiday-tour operator at the airport.

But luckily sharp-eyed Katie, whom Christine had written to and instructed what to expect, noticed the card and the woman and aimed her pointed face in that direction.

'Mrs Burton?' she said.

And Mrs Burton looked up.

Katie was quite taken aback to see the same expression of horror and recognition written on her new employer's face that she'd noticed on Christine's the day of the interview. Now what had she done wrong?

Mrs Burton still didn't say anything, and sharp-eyed Katie thought she saw a certain desolate misery in the lines on the woman's face. Katie put down her suitcase, she raised her skinny arm and rested her hand on Isobel's shoulder.

'Mrs Burton,' she said, 'Is there anything wrong?' Katie was genuinely concerned for her fellow human being, and I think it was the first time she'd felt that way for a very long time.

Isobel pulled her shoulder away and looked still more horrified. She started, and the common card fell from her hand to the floor. Katie made as if to pick it up, but then Mrs Burton spoke.

'A–Anna?'

Katie relaxed. She may have got the name wrong, but that could soon be sorted out. At least the woman could speak.

'Well, actually it's Katie, as a matter of fact – Katie Dye. I think I'm your new assistant manageress, or should I say housemaid?' She laughed.

'Katie?' said Isobel. '. . . Katie? . . .'

'That's right. Katie Dye.' Jesus, she'd come to live in a mad house.

'Katie. Welcome . . . well done . . .'

'What?'

Oh God.

Isobel still kept staring and even though Katie really was pretty desperate she was quite seriously tempted just to turn and run. She could honestly do without living with this.

Isobel pulled her shoulders up and made a big effort. But she couldn't stop staring. Just at the point when the whole situation was becoming totally impossible, Isobel managed to talk a bit of sense.

'The car's round the back. Let me take your case.'

'No, no, absolutely not. It's fine.' And Katie followed her employer off the platform to the front of the station. And Katie didn't notice Isobel's nonsense.

Katie was aware that there was something abnormal, if not yet unhealthy, in her eating habits, and although she doubted whether the loony would notice, she thought that she'd have to eat the lunch that Isobel had so earnestly offered her the moment they reached the Rectory.

When Katie said that, yes, she would love some lunch, Mrs Burton's face seemed to glow with pleasure. But when she added – for once truthfully – that she wasn't terribly hungry because she'd eaten a lot on the train, the woman's face had wilted once again.

They hadn't talked much on the journey home. At first they didn't talk at all. Isobel just drove blankly, and dangerously, in silence. Then Katie thought their lack of communication was a little embarrassing, seeing as the two of them were supposed to be about to 'build a life' together. So she asked Isobel about the hotel. How many rooms were there? What were the guests like? How many rooms were full at the moment? Etc., etc. Gradually, Isobel regained her composure. Maybe it was because she didn't have to look at Katie while they talked.

Isobel didn't ask Katie anything about her former life, or really anything about her at all. In a way, Katie liked the lack of nosiness that was so unusual with most grown-up women. But still, she enjoyed talking about herself even if it meant telling an awful lot of lies. So during the lunch (carefully prepared the night before by Christine), Katie steered the conversation around to herself. And to give her her due, she did it fairly gently.

'I used to live in Berkshire before I moved to London. I think Shropshire is such a beautiful county. The south is so horribly built up.'

But Isobel refused to talk about Katie's past. She refused to take it in, she wouldn't listen.

'Would you like some more salad?' she'd ask in reply.

'It's wonderful to be able to eat salad like this. When I was in London I just used to gorge myself on things like Chinese take-away and McDonald's hamburgers. I've got a terrible weakness for all those junk foods, I just can't stop my-self!'

Isobel looked up from her plate. She wasn't quite so stupid she couldn't recognise such an obvious anorexic's lie. She said, 'You certainly don't look as though you've been "gorging" yourself on anything of the kind. I'd say you needed to do a great deal more "gorging" before you even began to look healthy.'

Katie was surprised to be talked to so sharply by a stranger, and she was surprised by the amount of venom with which the whole spiel was delivered. Katie thought, if this woman weren't such a cripple I'd give her a tart remark back. But Katie took pity, which was probably just as well.

For a while they were silent. Then Katie started again. It was now almost a game to make Isobel show some sort of interest or comprehension of Katie's past.

'Do you keep horses here? I used to ride quite a bit as a child.'

'No, no horses. We've just got the dog now.'

'I used to have a lovely old dog when I lived at home, but it was run over.'

'We used to keep a cat, but he died some years ago, it was a great shame. The whole family was heartbroken.'

'Yes, in fact, although the dog was actually mine, my family was absolutely miserable the day it was killed.'

'No, I've never been tempted to ride at all; Anna used to ride when she was a little girl, such a sweet little pony . . .'

'My father refused to buy me a pony. He said I'd never bother to look after it propertly. It was probably the most sensible decision he made in his life.'

'We had to sell the pony in the end. I wonder where it is now. I dare say it's dead.'

And so it went on. Eventually Katie, most un-characteristically, admitted defeat. Anyway, the game was beginning to pall and she was supposed to be trying to get on with her employer. She asked about her duties and Isobel was vague.

'Oh, you know, just the sort of things that people do in hotels. To be honest, I don't really know much more about it than you do. Breakfast I suppose . . . it'd be nice if you could do that, and then beds and things, general tidying. I don't suppose you're any good at accounts?'

Katie was, so it looked like Isobel would really only have to give the occasional guided tour to sort out her finances. But Isobel is used to having things done for her, so maybe she doesn't appreciate Katie's goodwill and ability as much as she should.

As the two of them were clearing up lunch and Katie was feeling her enormous stomach, she remembered that the woman who'd interviewed her mentioned Isobel's being an artist.

'Is it true you paint?' she said.

Isobel looked up from the washing machine. 'Oh, I used to, but lately I don't seem to have done much at all. Perhaps now you're here to help me out I'll have a lot more time to myself. Yes. Maybe I'll start again. It used to be almost my *raison d'être* . . . maybe that was the problem.'

Katie listened and was about to ask what sort of painting Isobel did, but then she noticed the same mad, lost look on her face that had been there at the station.

'What was the problem, Mrs Burton?'

No reply.

'I've love to learn to paint properly,' she tried again. 'I'd love to learn how to use oils. Maybe one day I'll go to art school. Do you use oils, Mrs Burton?'

Isobel was back. 'Yes, absolutely always. When I was your age I used to paint the most ghastly, fey landscapes of the countryside in water-colours. Actually, they used to sell incredibly well. But the public are so ignorant . . . especially the ones with money.'

'Have you got any of your work here? It'd be great to see what sort of stuff you do.'

'Would it? Would you like that? Are you interested in art, Katie?'

It was the first time Isobel had admitted to knowing her name.

'Incredibly ignorant, but fascinated. You should start painting again. Apart from all the rest, I'd love to watch you working. There's something very beautiful about an artist at work.'

Katie winced when she took in what she'd just said. But for the first time since her arrival, Isobel had actually shown an interest in the newcomer. Katie was pleased, and in some lonely sort of way, rather touched. She hadn't wanted to lose her employer's attention; she'd overdone it.

Now Isobel, you may well have noticed, is not someone who takes kindly to nonsense such as that. And she suddenly looked disappointed. She knew that it was too early in their relationship to put her down, so she curbed her tongue (which was probably just as well).

Sharp-eyed Katie noticed Isobel's interest dim. 'Oh God, that sounds awful, what I really mean is, I'd love to watch you paint, then maybe I might be able to pick up a bit of technique.'

Isobel laughed. *Isobel laughed.* 'That sounds much better,' she said. 'Why don't you come to my studio and we'll have a look around.'

'Would you like to have a look at my etchings?' said Katie, and she thought it was rather a good joke. But for some reason Isobel didn't. She looked absolutely horrified, and Katie couldn't understand why. But she giggled nervously to cover her confusion and followed Isobel, who for once in her life was leading the way, into her studio.

The smell of turpentine seemed to bring Isobel a new lease of life. She hadn't been in the room since the builders had come, or maybe even before. It had been left absolutely untouched, as good Christine promised it would be.

Isobel brought out stacks of paintings that hadn't been touched for several years. It was a funny thing, but in the time that had passed since she'd last painted, Isobel had lost a great deal of her former confidence. That afternoon she *rediscovered her genius.* And Katie, apparently, discovered it for the first time too. She talked a lot about power and passion and I think what she said was genuine. Isobel certainly seemed to think so, and maybe that's all that really matters. Anyway, they stayed in the studio for several hours, only interrupted occasionally by telephone calls from clients wanting to book a room. Isobel talked more animatedly during those two hours than either Rufus or Christine had heard her talk for months, if not years.

I can't tell you what they said, because really it was just a lot of artistic nonsense that neither you (I hope) nor I could possibly understand or be interested in. But Katie was keen to learn. She asked a lot of pertinent questions that Isobel was only too happy to answer. By the end of the two hours, Katie had persuaded Isobel to take up her brush the very next day, and Isobel had persuaded Katie that there was nothing else in the world she would like to do more than teach her employee to paint.

But first Isobel had to get back into the swing of things. Lessons would begin next week. Isobel was looking forward to tomorrow, she really was.

After that they drank some tea. Katie took it without milk and Isobel's high spirits were dampened for a while. Then Katie was shown to her room. Christine thought it was only fitting that Katie should have the least saleable bedroom in the house, and that as you know, was Anna's. Katie was delighted by it, it was quiet and small and pretty, etc., etc. And Isobel didn't wonder why, but she didn't resent Katie's using it. In fact it rather pleased her. The room had been refilled as it was filled before, which in both cases was hardly very full at all.

Katie unpacked. She wasn't expected to do much work today. Anyway, most of the hotel's work happened in the morning.

It was six o'clock. Katie could do what she liked for the next two hours (she even had her own private bathroom), and at eight they were to meet in the kitchen for dinner. All very organised. Perhaps part of Christine has rubbed off on Isobel after all.

That evening the two of them continued their conversation

about art. Neither asked any questions about the other one's life, they both showed a remarkable lack of curiosity about their companion. Isobel and Katie are fairly secretive, unstraightforward people, and as soon as they both realised that they weren't going to have to spend a great deal of time evading questions, they relaxed in each other's company. Isobel said that on Friday she would take Katie to the local art shop and buy her a lot of expensive paints and paint brushes as a sort of welcoming present. Katie was embarrassed by the idea at first. But then she remembered her pathetic salary, and realised that there could be no question of her buying any equipment herself.

Isobel woke up early the next morning to the smells of bacon and eggs and toast. She was feeling over-excited and nervous at the prospect of the day ahead, but the smell made her hungry. She was about to put on one of Chrstine's awful frilly Marks and Spencer's shirts, when she remembered that nobody was there to frown if she didn't. So she put on her old paint-stained trousers and incredibly grubby shirt. And as she did so she felt a surge of warmth towards her new employee. But beyond that was only a blank. She enjoyed Katie's company and I think she genuinely liked her. But the girl's familiarity and her strangeness prevented Isobel from seeing her as an entity beyond what was immediately apparent.

Maybe I should make it clearer for those of you not paying full attention. Anna and Katie didn't only share the same disease. They also shared the same sharpness of feature and of mind. Anna's dark hair against her pale face and enormous blue eyes had perhaps been more striking than Katie's lighter colouring. But to Isobel the two of them seemed almost to merge as one. Remember, she'd never really studied her daughter and the starved, deceitful look of one anorexic is surprisingly similar to the look of another.

So Isobel went downstairs to the dining room and greeted her guests most graciously. The regulars (among whom the schoolmaster mentioned earlier, is one) thought she looked terrible that morning. Some of them knew her story, thanks to Christine, and they all thought, poor woman, she's already deteriorating now that Christine's left. The ghastly schoolmaster decided then and there that as a friend of the younger woman it was his duty to look after the older one. He would discuss what to do about the situation with his wife immediately after breakfast.

Isobel, unaware of the stir she'd caused that morning amongst her guests, wandered out of the dining room and straight into her studio. She hadn't yet stopped to think about *what* she was going to paint. In a highly unprofessional and optimistic way, she hoped it would just come to her in the half hour or so that she intended to spend mixing paints and setting up easels. Well, half an hour later, the paints, etc., were indeed beautifully set up. She even held a paintbrush in her hand. And she looked hopelessly at the blank canvas in front of her. She was totally lacking in inspiration that morning – or maybe it was altogether. She was just beginning to panic quite badly when Katie knocked on the door with a cup of coffee.

'How's it going?' she asked, a little bit too cheerfully.

Isobel looked up, relieved at the distraction. Katie was making her way round the easel to see how the work was progressing. When she saw, she couldn't hide her disappointment. She looked at the blank sheet of canvas for a couple of seconds in silence and then she just said, 'Oh.'

'What on earth am I to do? My mind is a total blank. There must be *something* to paint.'

'Oh dear, it's as bad as that, is it?' Katie was very familiar for an employee. Christine wouldn't have approved. But Isobel was far too distracted to notice, and anyway I've already explained, she finds it difficult to accept that that is the true sum of their relationship.

'Can't you just paint something from your imagination?'

'But that's just the problem. I don't know what's happened to my imagination!' Isobel sounded so desperate that for a moment Katie thought she might be going to laugh.

'OK then, why don't you paint something *not* from your imagination? Something real?'

'Like what? I suppose you want me to paint a bloody fruit bowl.'

'I don't see why not. But if that seems too boring, then you could always paint me.'

Isobel didn't look up from her blank canvas. 'Don't be silly, darling, you know I can't do portraits.'

Then she suddenly remembered who she was talking to. 'Oh dear, I'm sorry, Katie – of course you didn't know that. I think I thought you were someone else.' And then Katie saw the familiar blank misery pass over Isobel's face again. But she was more confident in her employer's company now, and although she had no understanding of what was troubling her, Katie did her best to shake her out of it.

'Come on,' she said. 'What's wrong with painting me? Just because you've never done portraits before, doesn't mean you can never do them. What's happened to your spirit of adventure?' Then Katie wondered if she'd gone too far. But no, old-fashioned Isobel still didn't seem to mind.

'Well, I don't know, now you come to think of it. It might be quite a challenge. I mean if you're willing . . . Of course, I'll pay you . . .'

'Definitely. Of course. Right, let's get moving.'

'Does three pounds an hour sound all right?' She was certainly a lot more generous than the other woman. 'Oh God, what about all the bloody beds and things?'

'Done them.' Katie understandably felt rather pleased with herself.

'Right then. Let's get moving.' If only her son could hear her sounding so positive. It would do him the world of good.

Isobel decided that there was very little point in Katie

wasting time just sitting for her. So she talked her model through every stage of paint mixing and canvas-preparing as they reached it. Katie listened hard and she learned a lot. She was dying for her own turn with the paint brush.

Meanwhile, the schoolmaster and his wife sat over elevenses in the guests' drawing room. They were worrying their beautifully trained, small, small minds about the state of Isobel's shirt cuffs. The wife, at least, showed a little room for compassion towards her good hostess.

'Poor woman,' she said. 'How did she ever let herself get like that? You'd think she didn't even want to look nice. No self-respect — *artists* . . . and then her daughter's dead. That must have been a blow, though I must say she doesn't exactly seem the maternal type. I wonder what her son's like. I wouldn't be surprised if he was a *homosexual* with a mother like that, and no father to keep a bit of discipline about the house. I think a young boy needs a father to teach him men's things . . .'

Her husband was about to interrupt her, and in fact he still did. But he let her finish the last bit. It made him feel *male*. And I hate to say it but schoolmasters often need idiotic wives to say idiotic things like that or they'd find it very difficult to survive as *men* outside in the real world.

'Jean,' he said, 'don't ramble. We are not discussing the sexual proclivities of our landlady's eldest son. We are discussing the speed of her deterioration since the departure of . . . the younger woman.'

The schoolmaster didn't like to call Christine by her Christian name, but he had very little choice because since the day of their arrival, she had refused to let him know what her other name was.

'Yes, of course, you're absolutely right. But what can we do? I wouldn't want her to think we were interfering. Maybe I could offer to do her laundry, but there's that thin new girl who must be paid to do that.'

'Don't be ridiculous. Of course you can't do her laundry. I will not be married to a washerwoman. I think you fail to understand that the state of her wardrobe is not the problem. It is the disposition of a person who is prepared to let herself fall to pieces like that. Mrs Burton's style of dress is merely a reflection of her state of mind. I think I should talk to her.'

That came as no surprise to his wife. There was really very little point in their discussing anything anyway. The schoolmaster always cut it short by saying in a suitably decisive and mysterious way that he would *talk* to the person concerned. Jean had no idea what actually went on during one of these talks. But when she heard those words she was comforted. She had the most extraordinary blind faith in her wise husband.

So the old schoolmaster left the dining room and went back up to their bedroom. He brushed what was left of his hair over his balding head and prepared what he was about to say.

He knocked on the studio door and Isobel was rather irritated. She was already quite absorbed in what she was doing.

'Come in.'

'Ah, Mrs Burton, I was wondering if you and I might have a little word –' he looked tactfully in the direction of the thin new housemaid – 'in private.'

Isobel was still more irritated. She'd never liked him much anyway. 'Anything you have to say can be said in front of Katie, too, you know. We are a partnership in this hotel.'

Katie felt herself blush. She was flattered.

The schoolmaster shifted his weight to the other sensibly shod foot. 'If you don't mind, Mrs Burton, what I have to say does not concern the young lady. I think it would be more comfortable for both of us if we could be alone.'

Then Isobel began to feel quite uncomfortable herself. And she certainly wasn't about to let Katie out now.

'I'm sure what you have to say can be said in front of all of us,' she said. She was beginning to sound rather like a schoolteacher herself.

He didn't know quite how to cope now. In his small world he was used to people jumping to his word. Only two pupils in his whole career had ever stood up against his wrath. And in both cases he carried the uncomfortable feeling that he had come out the loser. He looked around the room for a prop. There weren't any, just two pairs of hostile eyes staring at him and waiting for his reply. So he said, 'Very well' – I mean, he didn't have much choice.

Isobel waited, but he seemed to be at a loss for words. Neither she nor Katie felt the slightest temptation to help him along.

'Yes?' said Isobel.

And the schoolmaster took the plunge. 'It concerns your personal appearance, Mrs Burton. Various guests – and I include myself in their number – have expressed a certain amount of concern about your health.'

'*What?*' Isobel looked quite furious and quite amazed and almost as though she might be about to laugh. He did look absurd with his dignity, standing by the door.

'I was wondering if you might need a helping hand, a hand with all the work you have to do. Maybe you wanted a bit of help. After all, my wife has very little to do with her days. She was only just saying you might need a little help . . .' It was quite extraordinary how easily he crumpled.

'I do assure you that everything is strictly under control. But thank you so much for your kind offer. And now, as you say, I am a busy woman . . .'

'Yes, of course, I'm so sorry to have interrupted you, very busy, just to let you know that's all . . .' He was backing towards the door. 'I look forward to seeing the finished product,' he said, nodding his head towards Isobel's canvas, and he was gone.

Katie looked hard at the closed door and tried not to laugh.

She thought Isobel might be seriously angry. There was a moment's silence but then she heard the older woman's laughter and she relaxed. The one was as spiteful as the other. They were both lonely, too. Christine couldn't have known what a hit she'd scored.

CHAPTER 10

BUT KATIE STILL wasn't eating. Isobel was painting again and she smiled and she looked forward to tomorrow and she was in a muddle. Katie, in blissful ignorance, was happier than she had been for a long time and Isobel complimented her on her art. They spent long afternoons together in Isobel's studio. When she'd finished her portrait of Katie – about which more will be said later – she felt refreshed and she returned to her powerful abstracts. Meanwhile, Katie painted a fruit bowl.

Katie heard a lot about Rufus and still more about Anna. Rufus was in Thailand and his rather overbearing girlfriend was out of a job and living in London. Anna had rejected art as a young teenager, which was a shame because she'd shown a great deal of promise. But Isobel got her tenses muddled up and poor Katie had no idea that Anna was dead. In fact, she was rather looking forward to meeting her. Once she'd asked where Anna was now, and if she ever came home to Shropshire – that was about two weeks after she first arrived – but Isobel didn't hear and when Katie repeated the questions, Isobel's face showed again the dark misery that had troubled

Katie so much at the station. Isobel hadn't spoken for nearly half an hour after that, and Katie, who was a fast learner, had tried every trick she could to try and jerk her out of it. But all to no avail. Anyway, Katie didn't ask any more questions about Anna after that. She somehow sensed that Anna may have been at the root of her employer's problems, and she was very curious. But Katie knew she usually got her own way in the end, and she was fairly sure she'd get to the bottom of all the mystery before too long.

One day Isobel said to Katie, 'You know, you've got the same shaped face as Anna. When she was your age she used to cut her hair in this wonderful sort of bob. It was quite breathtaking. I was thinking if it suited her face, then there's no reason why it shouldn't suit yours.'

Katie was surprised. She looked up from the baked beans she was pushing around her plate. Isobel wasn't generally interested in things like haircuts.

'Yes,' she said, 'I've been meaning to get my hair cut for ages now; I never seem to get around to it.'

It was lunch-time. Isobel said, 'Let's go this afternoon. I think I might do something to my hair as well.'

Katie was embarrassed. She didn't like people making decisions for her but she didn't want to hurt Isobel's feelings. 'Actually, I haven't really got any money,' she said, 'and anyway, I'm dying to finish my fruit bowl. I've been thinking about it all morning.'

Isobel waved it all aside impatiently. 'Nonsense, I'll pay. After all, it's part of your job to look smart, didn't you listen to Christine at your interview?' They'd discussed Christine fairly unfavourably quite a lot. And Katie laughed at the element of spite in Isobel's words.

And it was decided. Katie had her hair cut according to Isobel's advice that afternoon and took her first unconscious steps towards feeding Isobel's lunatic fantasy. Isobel's fantasy was becoming a reality, but the haircut suited Katie and neither of them knew what they were doing. They returned to the studio with several hours before supper. Katie would be able to finish her fruit bowl after all.

Back in the studio the conversation turned to literature. Katie said that when she was at school she used to read a great deal but lately she didn't seem to be able to find the time, what with her new passion for painting and her job. Isobel listened carefully.

'Anna used to read a lot of Russian novels. Somewhere around there must be an absolute stash of them. I used to spend a fortune on them each time I went into Shrewsbury. Especially in the last few months . . . she didn't really have enough strength for anything else . . .' Isobel's mind began to wander again. She was lost in a world of her own that Katie was only just beginning to be able to understand. Katie chose her next words carefully.

'Was your daughter very ill?'

But Isobel didn't answer and Katie realised she would have to be still more patient. After several moments of silence Isobel suddenly asked:

'Do you ever read Tintin books at all?'

'I suppose I must have read a few when I was younger . . . Why? Do you?'

'You ought to. Anna used to read them all the time. I'll buy you some next time we go to Shrewsbury.

Katie thought it was all rather odd. She didn't particularly want any Tintin books but she said thank you all the same. She was never one to say no to presents.

Just then the telephone rang. It was Christine. She hadn't been down since Katie had arrived, although of course she'd spoken to Isobel several times on the telephone. Christine thought Isobel had sounded surprisingly cheerful on each occasion, and it rather annoyed her. Why was it that when everyone else was down and she was up she helped them, but when it was the other way around she was just left to rot? It was two months since Christine's return to London and she still hadn't found herself a job. The problem was, she was too proud. She'd been offered plenty of jobs in her field, but they all meant that she'd have to take a demotion, not to mention a salary drop. And Christine didn't want to work beneath people. The whole thing was a bit unfair, because she was good at her work and she was reliable, she just didn't have the necessary amount of charm to put herself back where she used to be. Anyway, the telephone rang and it was Christine who said she might pop down for the next couple of days, seeing as there was nothing much doing in London, and check out how things were going in the hotel.

Isobel tried to sound pleased and warm at the prospect. She also tried to dissuade her from coming.

'Everything's fine. Plenty of guests, Katie's a godsend, the money's rolling in. Don't worry about us, you stay up in London and have a good time, I'm sure you deserve it. We couldn't be coping better.'

Well, you can imagine that that was the last thing poor Christine wanted to hear. And she regarded the Rectory as home. She was lonely. But *still* she wanted her visit to seem like a favour.

'Look, I'd love to come down. It'd be nice to get out of London for a while and I'm sure you need a break. Absolutely no more discussion about it. I'll be there in time for supper tomorrow.'

Isobel's face fell and she made some fairly unconvincing warm reply. They said goodbye and Christine felt much better. She felt useful again.

Katie tried to feel as disappointed as Isobel sounded by the news of Christine's arrival. But she was so curious about the whole set-up at the Rectory and she thought she might be able to squeeze a few bits of information from the newcomer. Isobel talked for a while about how Christine had been very kind to the family at its time of need (Katie listened hard), but that she had to admit she found Christine very difficult to like. She was bossy and overbearing. Katie kept quiet, but from her short experience of Rufus's girlfriend, she found she couldn't have agreed more.

Isobel put down her paintbrush and covered up her powerful piece of work. It was supper time. Every day the meals grew more and more starch-filled and fattening. It was a desperate attempt on Isobel's part to fatten up her new daughter. But for all her experience in the anorexic field, she still had a sad lack of understanding about the way it worked.

Katie had developed a lot of tricks and, whatever the food, very little of it ever reached her stomach. She pushed the food into compact heaps on her plate so that what she'd really left there seemed much less than it actually was. She hid food under her knife and fork, and of course where it was possible she slipped a certain amount under the table and fed it to the dog. She ate a bit and on the occasons she ate any more than a bit she sicked it up. Katie was very thin, as she had been when she first arrived. But she doesn't seem to have lost much weight since her arrival at the Rectory. Maybe that's because once you reach a certain level of thinness, any thinner just looks the same.

So the two of them ate supper and Katie played all her old tricks. And Isobel noticed, as she always did and she talked hard to try and cover it. But she found it very painful. She tried to block the problem out of her mind, which is exactly what she did with Anna and that didn't get her very far. It looked like history was about to repeat itself. If only Isobel could see.

The next day Katie didn't find Isobel in the studio as she usually did. The car was gone so she must have gone out. At lunch-time Isobel returned. She was carrying an enormous cardboard box with some difficulty and she looked rather pleased with herself. Katie was surprised by how happy she felt to see Isobel again. She'd been vaguely worrying about her all morning.

'I've bought you some presents,' Isobel said. 'I think I've been to every single bookshop in Shrewsbury. Have a look inside there.' She nodded in the direction of the box that was by now resting on the kitchen table.

Katie moved awkwardly towards the box. She thought she knew what would be inside. And she was more or less right. There were three paperback Russian novels, all of which Katie had read, but she was kind enough not to mention that fact, and there were seventeen different Tintin adventures, none of which Katie had read and none of which she thought looked in the least bit interesting.

Isobel stood expectantly, waiting for Katie's cries of delight. But none came.

Isobel's face dropped. 'Well?' she said. 'Aren't you pleased? You were saying only the other day how much you loved Tintin. Well, now you can read about him to your heart's content. Look, I've even bought you a book about Hergé's life.' Isobel scrambled through the ridiculous heap of new books and brought out the one about Hergé.

Katie felt more than uncomfortable. She remembered the conversation Isobel was referring to quite clearly. *She* had barely expressed an opinion about Tintin at all. But maybe she was making too much of it. Isobel was forgetful and she'd gone out of her way to please Katie when there was absolutely no necessity for her to do so. Katie didn't want to hurt Isobel's feelings. And anyway, it couldn't do any *harm* to be the possessor of seventeen Tintin adventures and the story of the life of the author. At last Katie smiled. And it was a genuine smile.

'Of course I'm pleased. They're wonderful. I love Tintin and I love sets. Thank you very much.' Katie held each book and looked at it for the appropriate amount of time and with the appropriate amount of seeming pleasure, and then she took them up to her room.

When she returned to the kitchen Isobel seemed to be in lower spirits than usual. She'd remembered Christine's arrival and all that it would entail. For a start she would have to change back into her Marks and Spencer's respectable gear. All very depressing, and I think not entirely dignified. After lunch Isobel changed as she thought she should and for the rest of the afternoon Katie thought she was not herself at all. She seemed to be rather jittery, and not even Isobel, had she stopped to think, could have worked out why. Isobel was sure that Christine would bring disruption. She was bound to disapprove of something. Isobel had the faint, unconscious feeling that she'd done wrong. But she couldn't work out how.

Christine arrived at the Rectory in time for supper and she carried with her the usual pasta from her local Italian shop. They sat down almost immediately to eat. Isobel had roasted a chicken, which was quite a surprise to Christine in itself. Christine asked Katie how she was getting along, and when that topic ran out she asked her what A levels she'd been taking before she left school. Katie was quite sullen again. Sullen like she used to be at home.

Christine exaggerated the fun she'd been having in London since she'd last been down and Isobel and Katie made polite noises. Then she talked about Rufus and the two of them showed a little more interest. Right now he was in Melbourne.

Christine noticed that Katie Dye had certainly not put on any weight since the interview and she watched her pushing the chicken around her plate in a most unattractive and familiar way. Still, it had to be said that Isobel was blooming. Christine hadn't seen her looking so well for maybe a year. But she noticed that Isobel never once looked Katie in the eye during dinner. Christine thought, surprisingly enough, that the situation called for action.

Immediately after dinner Isobel said she was exhausted and that she was going to bed. Both Katie and Christine were pleased by the news. Christine wanted to have a little talk and Katie was finding it almost impossible to control her curiosity about the general set-up any longer. Most of all she wanted to know about Anna.

Whe Isobel left the room both Christine and Katie offered the other a cup of coffee. They were frightened that the other might decide to go to bed too. Christine stood with her back to the room. She was filling the kettle. And she began.

'Katie, I don't know exactly how much you understand about the Burtons. I mean, do you know anything about them at all? Isobel's never been particularly open with anyone, but the two of you do seem to get on well.'

Katie didn't know quite what to say. She saw that this was the chance she'd been waiting for and she didn't want to blow it. She thought the best idea would be to keep quiet. So she did.

Christine switched on the kettle and turned around. She looked at the younger girl reflectively and waited. Katie looked at the floor and she said, 'Well, no, I mean, I don't think I know much about them. Except that the father's dead and that you're Rufus's um . . .'

Christine didn't notice Katie's embarrassment. She interrupted before the 'um' would have been noticeable. 'Do you know about Anna?'

'Well, it depends what about Anna. Yes I know a bit about her, silly things like she likes Tintin books.'

'Did she? Well, that's not particularly useful. What I'm trying to ask is whether or not Isobel has told you how she died.'

Katie didn't understand. 'How she *died*?'

'Mmmm . . . Yes, did she?'

'For Christ's sake, I didn't even know she was *dead* . . . I knew there was something about her. I mean I knew this family had problems and I thought she might have been at the root of them . . . Christ . . . *dead*. Why didn't she tell me?'

145

A bit of drama. Christine was shocked, but at last she was enjoying herself.

'Sit down, Katie,' she said, 'I think it's time you and I had a little talk.'

So at last Katie's curiosity was satisfied. And Christine didn't spare her one gory little detail. Katie's senses were slightly numbed by the horrible story, and she was seeing how so many things made sense that before she had been unable to understand.

Christine wondered whether or not to go any further. She decided that having Katie alone like this and with her full attention was an opportunity not to be missed. Anyway, Katie's recovery was, as far as Christine was concerned, the whole point of Katie's existence in their lives. So she went further.

'Having said that, Katie, perhaps you will excuse me if I make a few comments about your role in this saga. I chose you for this job because you seemed to be the best suited of all the girls for the job. And it seems to me that I have clearly made the best choice. Isobel's much better since you arrived – she's even started painting again. But – and I must be frank with you – it is unfortunate and absolutely undeniable that you and Isobel's late daughter are clearly suffering from the same disease. I was hoping that your health and general appearance might have improved a little after two months with plenty of distractions and good old-fashioned country air. When I met you at the interview you had the air of a survivor about you. But you look much the same if not worse than you did before. Now, believe it or not, I know more about anorexia than you do . . .'

Katie smothered a slightly hysterical giggle, it made her think of the cross-your-heart bra advertisement.

'Katie, I don't think I'm lacking in a sense of humour, but I find it very difficult to see what's so funny about this conversation.'

Katie felt like a schoolgirl. 'No, no of course there isn't. You must made me think of that bra advertisement, believe it or not, we know more about . . .'

'Oh for God's sake, I thought I was talking to an adult, will you grow up and listen?'

Under any other circumstances, Katie would have rather lost her cool at being talked to like that by anyone, let alone by a relative stranger whom she didn't like anyway, but this time she was interested in what Christine had to say, although the whole thing about her eating habits always made her feel uncomfortable. So she just said sorry and waited for Christine to continue, and she had no doubt that she would.

Which of course she did.

'Now, what I'm about to say may perhaps sound rather harsh to you, but I'm a great believer in honesty, and maybe it might even do you some good. I know that an anorexic's obsession with her body and with food goes far beyond reason or logic. I also know that the whole thing is not only obsessive but *self*-obsessive. Maybe you're too young, maybe you're too selfish, but in as much as I can see anything – and I pride myself, and I hope you will agree, on being fairly sensitive to my surroundings – as far as I can see you and Isobel have grown really quite fond of one another. I would say that you genuinely get along rather well. Would you agree?'

'Yes, I think so, we have a certain amount in common.' Katie tried to hide the fact that she was flattered. She was never sure whether or not Isobel liked her at all.

'I think you're probably old enough to have some understanding of how much this family – particularly Isobel – has suffered in the past few months.'

Katie's attention was beginning to wander. She'd found out all she wanted to know and at the moment she was too preoccupied about that to listen to Christine's comments about her age. She started to fiddle with the packet of Silk Cut on the table and look at the clock on the wall. She even yawned.

She wanted to be left alone. Christine noticed and she wondered whether it was worth carrying on. Katie was quite clearly not in a very receptive mood, and Christine was working around asking her for an impossible favour. She was trying to ask whether or not Katie could possibly cure herself of a disease that as yet she wasn't even able to accept that she suffered from, in order to make Isobel's life a little easier. Well, that's an over-simplification but it gives the general idea. It was a big request, and to be honest a rather un-imaginative one. Christine clearly didn't understand Katie's problem as well as she thought she did.

Anyway, she looked at Katie fidgeting and thought that perhaps now wasn't the time. So she offered Katie another cup of coffee and in the same breath said she was exhausted and wanted to go to bed.

Katie leapt on the idea and very soon afterwards the two of them went their separate ways.

That night Katie thought a lot about what Christine had told her. So Anna was dead. It was a shock. In a funny sort of way she thought she might have found a kindred spirit in the dead daughter. She thought of Isobel and of Isobel's guilt. And that night she cried for someone else. It was a quite a breakthrough.

The next morning two things of consequence happened at the Burton household. And both of them involved Christine.

Firstly, she took Isobel aside and told her that she had to face facts and that nice and good though Katie was, she was ill and she needed help before it was too late. For the first time since Christine had known her, Isobel lost her temper. Did Christine think she was blind? Did she think Isobel couldn't see what was going on right beneath her nose? And what the hell had Christine thought she was doing hiring another case to look after the hotel anyway? Hadn't she been through enough already?

Christine was amazed by the outburst. And what she said

in reply to it couldn't possibly have been more irritating if she'd tried.

'I'm very glad to see all your aggression come to the surface like this,' she said. 'I'm glad to see that you still have a fighting spirit. You should put it to good use. Persuade Katie to see a doctor. I swear to you, if she gets better it won't only be to *her* advantage.'

Isobel listened and when Christine had finished she couldn't think of anything suitably crushing to reply. So she made an odd frustrated grunting noise and walked angrily out of the room. She slammed the door like a child.

Christine lit herself a cigarette and wasn't in the least embarrassed at upsetting her hostess. She thought it was all in a good cause, which of course if it works out, would make her absolutely right.

The other occurrence that morning caused great pleasure to three people at the Rectory and only a certain disappointment for one. The schoolmaster was sad that Christine would be rushing back to *town*, as he called it, so soon after her arrival. He hadn't had a chance for a proper conversation.

Someone rang Christine – apparently an old friend – to tell her about a job that she might be interested in. This time it had nothing to do with contacts. The man who was calling had read about it that morning in the *Guardian*, he knew she was getting pretty desperate (whoops) and he wanted to be sure that she didn't miss it. Christine sounded very relaxed about the whole thing on the telephone, but as soon as she'd said goodbye she began to make enquiries. It turned out she would have to return to London that evening in order to be interviewed the next morning.

Katie and Isobel wished her good luck and said they looked forward to her coming down again soon. Then Isobel went up to her bedroom and changed out of her sensible clothes. Isobel wondered for a while if she hadn't been a little *too* unfriendly. After all, Christine had done an awful lot for her.

But then she moved into her studio and soon forgot every-thing apart from her powerful art.

That afternoon Katie was painting a jug. She may have been absorbed in what she was doing, but as she overheard a certain amount of what passed between Isobel and Christine that morning, I would say that she had other things on her mind. Isobel didn't talk much to her companion, either. Her art was all-consuming or so she hoped it might appear. Actually, what Christine had said that morning had disturbed her a great deal. She wondered about Katie, and she knew something ought to be done. Up until then she hadn't fully admitted to herself what was wrong, but when Christine confirmed her greatest fears she knew that this was her second chance. She saw quite clearly that she didn't want to blow it again. But perhaps they were all wrong. Perhaps they were just hysterical. Not every thin girl was a mad woman for God's sake, and anyway maybe the problem would just go away. Maybe she was getting better anyway. And who was she to interfere? Katie didn't make her wear smart clothes, why should she be able to make her eat? – and so on. But she didn't say anything. Not this afternoon anyway. She must give herself some time to think things out.

At supper Isobel watched Katie's plate nervously. She didn't want Katie to see her watching. Katie played with her food even more than usual. Everyone was being quite hysterical. There was absolutely nothing wrong with her, but she didn't want to upset Isobel. She tried to hide her food even more skilfully than usual. And to give her her due, she probably ate a couple more mouthfuls than was normal as well. It was a tense and silent evening. Almost as bad as that first drive from the station to the Rectory the day after Katie arrived.

Both Katie and Isobel said they were unaccountably tired that evening, and they both went to bed at the earliest reason-able opportunity.

Neither of them slept much that night. Katie lay awake in

Anna's bed thinking, 'This is Anna's room, this is her bed and she's dead and everybody thinks I'm going the same way.' Katie felt her jutting hips and her swollen appendix and for the first time since the whole ghastly thing had begun, they didn't give her any pleasure. Suddenly they felt grotesque and suddenly she was frightened. She thought of Anna feeling her hips and she thought of Anna dead. Katie certainly didn't want to die. The thought had never occurred to her before. She turned over but, like the princess and the pea, the buttons on her old-fashioned mattress dug into her and it hurt. She had bruises all over her body from the buttons on the mattress. She wasn't comfortable and she knew she wouldn't sleep. She switched on the light and reached for one of the Tintin books. She read three that night.

The next morning Isobel slept late, but poor Katie had to get up to cook bacon and make polite conversation to the schoolmaster and the likes.

As she put the bacon and the Frank Cooper's marmalade in front of the schoolmaster, he said, 'You could do with eating up a bit of this yourself, young lady. Girls these days think it's so fashionable to be thin. If you ask me it's unattractive. Men like their women with curves. There's nothing attractive about a stick.' He laughed, unaware of the offence he had caused.

Katie didn't reply. She wanted to throw the Frank Cooper's marmalade all over his face, but she didn't have the energy or the strength. Fuck him and his curves. Instead she gave him a piercing look and walked out of the room. The schoolmaster laughed and he said to his wife, 'Young people must learn not to fly off the handle so easily. Discipline.'

The wife agreed.

Isobel and Katie avoided each other that morning. Once Isobel got up, she went straight outside. She left a message on the kitchen table saying she'd taken the dog for a walk and that she'd be back for lunch.

Katie was quite pleased by the message, and she'd worked out a plan to put Isobel's mind at ease about her health which also stopped Katie from having to put on more weight in the process. No, she didn't want to get any thinner, but she certainly didn't want to get fat. So, of course, she couldn't eat at all.

Lately, Katie had been trying to cut down on the vomiting. She knew it really couldn't be doing her any good, but right now she knew it could be the only answer to her problems. So she'd eat plenty in front of her boss, so she'd sick it up again behind her back and life would be peaceful once again – like it was before Christine came and disrupted their happy equilibrium.

At lunch, Isobel watched Katie wolfing down her food and when Katie excused herself before the coffee to go to the lavatory, Isobel followed her. She heard her retching into the bowl and she knew she couldn't keep quiet any longer. She tiptoed back to the kitchen and sat back down at the kitchen table. Her heart was beating incredibly fast. But for once, like Christine, she knew some facts had to be faced.

Katie came back into the room looking only slightly shirty. She sat down and coughed and looked around for something to put into her mouth to cover the smell of vomit on her breath. Isobel watched her, but still in silence.

'Katie, I know you've just thrown up your lunch.' Isobel was trembling.

Katie opened her eyes wide, wide, wide, she was a practised deceiver, but she couldn't stop herself from blushing, or from dropping the piece of bread she was about to put into her mouth.

'What?' she said. 'Why on earth would I do a stupid thing like that?'

'Don't lie to me, I've been lied to before. I *heard* you retching.'

'You're going mad.'

'Don't speak to me like that. How dare you tell me I'm going mad. You're the mad one. You're mad, do you hear? You're mad. Mad! Mad! Mad!' Her voice was rising hysterically, and Katie just sat opposite her looking blank.

'Do you hear me? You're mad,' she shouted. But still no reaction. Katie was silent.

'MAD.'

A moment's silence and the two women looked at each other. On Katie's part she felt no hostility. Just a great sadness. She saw that her presence was causing a certain amount of suffering. She didn't want to hurt her friend. But Isobel had eating problems on her mind. If Katie stuck around here she'd be turned into a football. No, she had to be moving on. But where to she had no idea, nor did she give it a moment's thought as she pushed back her chair and moved towards the door.

'It's no good, I don't want this, I'll go and pack my bags.'

Isobel leapt up from her chair and grasped Katie by the top of her arm. For a second Isobel thought it might be going to snap.

'No! . . .' They looked at each other again. Katie was waiting for Isobel to carry on. Isobel was crying, she shook the scraggy arm. 'No, you're not going. You will stay here and work for me and I will pay for you to visit a psychiatrist . . . *please.*'

Katie saw her desperation and her misery and of course she understood their strength. She didn't actually formulate these words in her head but she thought that as far as Isobel was concerned, Katie knew nothing about her late daughter. If Isobel wasn't prepared to give everything to the situation then why should Katie even consider it? She was hurt that even now Isobel couldn't face her with the truth. There was a moment's silence and Katie looked her employer straight in the eyes.

'I'm leaving.' She tried to escape from Isobel's hold, but

she was weak and she failed; it took away from the finality of her words.

Isobel tightened her hold. Her face crumpled and she began to sob like a child.

'My daughter . . . don't you see . . . you can't leave . . . not now.'

'What about your daughter, Mrs Burton?' Katie's voice was cold and in horrible control.

Isobel's head was stooped and she covered her face with her free hand. Katie waited. It was Isobel's last chance. She repeated the question.

'What about your daughter, Isobel? What happened to your daughter?'

Isobel kept her head low and what she said was muffled by her tears and her hand.

'She died.'

Katie didn't move and she didn't say anything. Isobel's sobs turned to wails.

'SHE DIED.' And she shouted it this time, and her head was raised level.

Suddenly Katie's control left her, and the force of her compassion came back. She couldn't bear to see this woman's misery and know that she played some part in it. For a moment she thought of her mother and she wondered if she'd caused the same anguish at home. She hadn't died, but to them she was as good as dead. She wanted to pay back something of what she owed, and it was too late to do that to her own mother. She wanted to comfort this surrogate mother, and she knew there was only one way to do it.

'I know, I know she died. I think I've known for a long time, I think I've always known it. And I know why she died and I know why I'm here and I know I'm ill and I'd like you to help me – if you can. Or even if you want to, I don't know that I deserve it. I don't know who else can help me . . . I . . . don't know who else. I'm very alone here, I . . .'

And now it was Katie's turn to cry. She too covered her face with her free hand. Isobel watched in amazement. She heard Katie's muffled apology and she put her arm round her and led her back to her chair.

'No, don't cry, don't apologise. It's not your fault any more than it is mine. Don't apologise. You couldn't help it. I couldn't help it. Don't apologise, everything's going to be all right from now on. You'll see. We'll get you better, you can see a doctor, it still isn't too late. By the end of six months you'll look like a new girl.'

Katie was still crying. You see, she didn't ever want to look like a new girl. She didn't want to get better, but she couldn't possibly admit it. She didn't want to put on any more weight. She *didn't want help*. She just wished she could stay thin and Isobel could be made to feel happier. But she would go to the psychiatrist. Perhaps he would be able to persuade them that there was nothing wrong. Poor Katie. Poor, poor Katie.

Eventually her crying died down and Isobel slipped into another room to make enquiries about psychiatrists. This time she would hire the very best and this time she won't have acted too late.

★   ★   ★

So Katie kept her appointments with the local psychiatrist – Isobel had left instructions that if Katie proved too big a problem then the local psychiatrist was to refer her to a specialist – and Isobel bloomed.

In actual fact Katie began to put on weight after the scene in the kitchen too. She began to eat . . . and eat . . . and eat. Most of her eating was done in secret, but she wasn't sick afterwards. She just hated herself with an ever growing passion. She wouldn't allow herself to be sick because she wanted to punish herself for being so self-indulgent as to have eaten so much in the first place. Every day she used to wake up vowing to her aching swollen stomach that she'd starve it that day, but somehow she couldn't even last beyond breakfast. When she was very full and feeling sick she used to force more down her throat. Everyone thought he was, but her psychiatrist wasn't helping a bit. She ate as a punishment. Her old, manic willpower had evaporated. And Katie was very unhappy.

Her face grew unhealthily puffy and her stomach stuck out like a balloon. But her chest stayed flat and her legs and arms still looked like sticks. And she still didn't have a period. She hadn't bled for at least two years but it didn't worry her too much, after all babies were a long way off.

So Isobel walked tall and told Katie over and over again how much better she looked, and Katie cried herself to sleep with self-hatred every night.

The schoolmaster, who thought he was on very good and familiar terms with the household, told Katie he was pleased she'd taken heed of his advice and he patted her bottom – his wife wasn't in the room and he felt very daring and masculine. Katie spun round and glared at him. She said, 'Don't you dare touch my bottom,' and stormed up to her bedroom where she burst into tears. And stared at her reflection in the mirror and pinched her new flesh with a venom so that it hurt.

Katie hated herself so she tried to make herself look as ugly as she possibly could – although it wasn't exactly conscious. She wore the same very baggy trousers and jersey every day because she thought they covered her repulsive body and she let her hair hang flat and dirty on her head.

Even her new passion for painting suffered from her state of mind. She couldn't bring herself to try. She painted badly because she didn't want to do it well, and she carried on visiting her psychiatrist. But she never told him anything but lies. She still couldn't understand what she was doing to herself. And she wanted to go back to the way she was. At least she didn't resent Isobel, or the part she'd played in the gaining of her new fat. All her passion and her hatred was directed against herself.

★　　★　　★

Lately Isobel had taken to calling Katie 'darling' and Katie didn't call Isobel anything. Isobel brought out all her photographs of Anna back into public view and to Katie she would talk about nothing else. One day, as they painted side by side in her studio, Isobel said to Katie that she been thinking, Katie seemed to show a sadly restricted wardrobe, judging by the way she dressed. She said it seemed a shame to waste Anna's beautiful clothes, that she – Isobel – couldn't possibly fit into them. Why didn't she bring them all out and let Katie take her pick of what she liked?

Now Anna had had the most beautiful and expensive collection of clothes. They made Katie quite think of her earlier days, and she was excited at the sight of them. She picked out a pair of suede jodhpur trousers that must have set the buyer back by Katie's annual salary. And as she went to try them on, she knew her waist wouldn't be able to fit into them. Still, she wanted to show herself, so she tried and sure enough she couldn't do them up.

She rejoined Isobel and the pile of clothes carrying the trousers over her arm. Her face was long. 'Actually, I don't think they really suit me,' she said. 'What else is there?'

Isobel looked disappointed. She said, 'Darling, I remember Anna wearing them and they looked beautiful on her. Go and try them on again.'

'No,' Katie snapped, but then she felt guilty. After all, how was Isobel to know? So she added, 'I don't think I'd ever feel comfortable in them.'

Isobel sighed. Katie didn't make the mistake of trying on

157

any other clothes that might make contact with her waist. But she took a lot of baggy – very expensive – jerseys and jackets and shirts. She and Anna even had the same size feet and Isobel didn't seem to think sharing shoes was unkosher, so Katie took a lot of grand and elegant shoes away – back to Anna's room – with her, too.

Isobel was enjoying herself. She said she'd kept some of Anna's old jewellery as well. She even had Anna's old bottle of Opium.

Katie took most of the jewellery but she thought the scent really was going too far. She said the scent had gone off and threw it away before Isobel had the chance to argue.

Isobel watched the bottle fall into the dustbin with a blank, glazed sort of look. Then she said in a mechanically cheerful voice:

'Never mind, darling, I'll buy you another bottle when I next go into Shrewsbury. Would you like that?'

And poor Katie didn't know what to say.

CHAPTER 11

CHRISTINE DIDN'T GET the job that was advertised in the *Guardian*. They said she didn't have enough diversity of experience because she'd only ever worked in one firm. In her heart of hearts Christine knew it was unfair and wrong, but she was beginning to wonder all the same. Perhaps she should branch out into something totally different. Or perhaps she should forget all her dreams of being a high-powered career woman and just settle down and make a family. She was shocked at how tempting it seemed.

Rufus was coming home after his three months of absence and Christine was in quite a dither. She'd avoided all conversation about herself during their brief telephone conversations while Rufus was away. And she didn't know quite how she was going to account for the last three months. Her three months of failure. In fact she wasn't even sure if she was looking forward to seeing him again. Things would have been so much better if she could greet him with the knowledge that she was impressively employed – or even employed at all.

On Rufus's aeroplane the light had just come up telling him to stub out his cigarette and fasten his seat belt. He was looking suntanned and healthy and he'd grown a beard. Rufus could barely sit still he was feeling so nervous. He thought he was dying to see Christine again. But he'd sensed a certain dissatisfaction in her when he called. And now he came to think of it he didn't even know if she'd found a job. Well, she would have been bound to, but it was funny she hadn't mentioned it. In a way he rather hoped she hadn't found a job, however unlikely that may be. Then it might be slightly easier to persuade her that it was time they thought of making a family.

Christine had another seven stops on the tube before she reached Heathrow. She would arrive perfectly on time.

Rufus picked up all his luggage and came through the gate. They saw each other at the same time and they ran into each other's arms. They both talked a lot at the same time, and Christine nearly cried. Rufus said, 'Let's get a taxi back to London,' which was very extravagant but Christine agreed.

In the taxi Rufus opened up every one of his suitcases and from them poured endless useless and beautiful gifts on his girlfriend. Lace and silk and pearls and precious jewels and a Pentax camera from Hong Kong and four hundred cigarettes and an enormous bottle of Chanel No. 5. Christine laughed and laughed and her silly eyes grew damper and damper as more and more presents were piled high on to her lap. Rufus hadn't drawn breath since they'd met, and so far Christine hadn't had to tell him any of her news, and she preferred it that way.

Christine looked down at her bounty and said that Rufus's return was a present in itself and that he needn't have brought her all this.

'Ah, but hang on, I still haven't finished. There's still one more present to come, if only I could find it . . . I don't know if it's really your thing, I mean if it isn't . . . it was an impulse buy.' He rummaged around a bit more.

'Here it is.' He brought out a small square, leather box and handed it to Christine.

Christine's heart had stopped beating. She knew what would be inside and she knew that it would be *absolutely* her thing.

She took the box in silence and she fumbled with the catch. Rufus looked on expectantly. Inside was a second-century Roman coin, a very interesting specimen.

'Well?' said Rufus. 'Do you like it? I know you don't collect coins, but I thought it was so beautiful and you'll never believe how cheap it was, although I suppose I shouldn't say that . . .' He smiled.

Christine's earlier euphoria and her face collapsed. 'Oh Rufus,' she said, 'it's lovely.'

Rufus didn't notice his terrible *faux pas* and he began to tell Christine about the beautiful way oriental girls dressed and how it was a shame that western girls always had to look so scruffy. Why was it that western fashions designed clothes to hide women's figures? Christine wasn't feeling strong enough to tell him to belt up. She didn't want them to argue so soon after they had met.

But as it turned out they argued before they reached home anyway. Once they'd stuffed all Rufus's belongings back into the cases he took time off to ask after Christine.

'So tell me all about the new high-powered job you've been keeping so quiet about since I left.'

It was quite an annoying way to put it even under the best of circumstances. Christine thought his tone was rather patronising and I would be prone to agree with her.

She was feeling let down over the Roman coin saga anyway, and she'd allowed him the oriental girl nonsense. Christine isn't a great one for holding her tongue. And the question made her feel uncomfortable.

'Don't be so bloody patronising.'

Rufus was surprised. 'Oh God, I'm sorry, Chris, it wasn't meant to come out that way. You just haven't told me any news about yourself at all. What have you been up to all this time, apart from sleeping with all my best friends?' He laughed – trying to lighten the atmosphere.

Well, that was pretty patronising too.

'Don't be patronising, darling, I'm not a child. And if you really want to know I haven't done much. I didn't hear once from your Australian – apart from on the day you left when he rang to check you'd got off all right. I think he could have asked me out to dinner once at least.'

Rufus didn't agree, after all Arthur was his friend and his business associate. He had nothing to do with Christine at all. And anyway Rufus sensed that he and Christine wouldn't exactly have got along. But he kept quiet.

There was a silence in the cab and then Christine continued. 'And I haven't got a job. I haven't really been looking though. I was thinking of branching out into something completely different. I mean if *you* can do it then there's no reason why I can't.'

For some reason Rufus wasn't feeling so entirely warm towards his girlfriend now as he had been during their three months' separation, and when he heard that Christine was out of work he wasn't so attracted to the idea of marriage as he thought he would have been. Well, he certainly wasn't in the mood for a proposal now anyway. And he thought Christine didn't seem to be either – if she ever was.

Rufus tried to sound enthusiastic. 'Absolutely, why not? What sort of work did you have in mind?'

'I don't know yet, I haven't thought about it. God Rufus, you sound like a bloody careers officer. Can't we just relax on your first day home and not worry about the future for once? Tell me about New York.'

Rufus told Christine about New York and Christine didn't

listen. She was wondering why she had to be so unpleasant to the one person she loved when he'd only been warm to her and when they hadn't seen each other for so long. She wondered how she would be able to make it up to him.

The taxi drew up outside their flat and they squabbled a bit about who should pay the driver. Christine won, which meant she paid, and for some reason that put her in a better mood.

Christine had cooked a lot of *ratatouille* and other good things for lunch to welcome Rufus home. Rufus failed to hide his disappiontment. He'd been looking forward to taking Christine out somewhere really good with his newly earned fortune. He said, 'Oh how delicious,' in a flat voice and consoled himself that he'd be able to take her out to dinner.

Just as they were sitting down to lunch the telephone rang. Christine answered and Rufus could tell by the chill in her voice that it must be Arthur. He sheepishly took the receiver from Christine and prepared his smoothest manner for the man he was about to talk to. The Australian wanted to meet Rufus that evening for a business dinner. Rufus knew anyway that he had the permanent job offered beforehand, but details had to be discussed. And Arthur would not be swayed. It seemed that it was absolutely impossible for them to meet at any other time. Well, Christine would just *have* to understand. After all, it was his career that was at stake. But still, he didn't relish the idea of breaking the news to her and judging by the look on her face already, she'd picked up most of what was going on anyway. He hung up.

'So I gather you're going out to dinner without me this evening?'

'Em, ya. But you heard me, Chris, I tried my hardest to get out of it, didn't I, and you know what he's like . . .'

'No, I don't actually. Perhaps it's about time I did. How do you know he isn't queer, for God's sake?'

'Well, he isn't and even if he was, what would it matter anyway?'

163

'Of course it doesn't matter. But it's a bit suspect him ringing you up within seconds of your getting home and then forcing you to have a tête-à-tête dinner with him alone.'

'Oh don't be a baby, Christine.'

It seems to me that their roles have reversed. This sweet relationship must be doomed. Christine put down her knife and fork and walked with the utmost dignity out of the room. How dared he talk to her like that!

Rufus sat alone in front of his cooling *ratatouille* and lit himself a cigarette. His great reunion had been a bit of an anticlimax. He looked across at the pile of presents bought with such goodwill. They lay sourly on top of the dresser. He sighed. What on earth had got into her? She was not the same woman he had left behind.

But Rufus wasn't a man — and which one is? — to spend much time worrying about the root of a problem. He just wanted to smooth things out as quickly and as easily as possible. He felt quite hurt and quite sad. Perhaps she'd been having too good a time while he was away. Of course, the best thing to do would be to apologise — although what exactly for, Rufus wasn't absolutely sure.

After a while he followed her into the bedroom. Christine was sitting on the bed with a cigarette in her hand and had quite clearly been waiting for him.

'I'm sorry I called you a baby, darling. And you know how I feel about this evening. I want us to be together just as much as you do.' He was learning her language. *What* would Isobel say?

He put his arm around her and Christine moved away.

Well, he went on coaxing and wheedling and Christine carried on answering in sensitive monosyllables until he began to feel a bit irritated himself. Just at the point where he might have lost his cool, Christine decided to relent. They made a superficial pretence at friendship and Rufus felt relieved. Then they made love, which was what the whole thing had been leading up to anyway, but they both still carried a certain

164

bitterness in their hearts against the other.

Afterwards, as they say, Rufus tried to discuss Christine's career again. But she evaded the issue again, and Rufus felt the beginnings of yet another fight, so he decided to drop it.

Rufus came home early from dinner with the Australian, as he promised he would, and for the next couple of days he and Christine got along fairly well. Rufus would be starting work at Arthur's London headquarters in a week's time. So after three days in London, the couple decided to go up to Shropshire. Rufus planned to spend the weekend in the country and then go back down to London and party-party.

On the way up to Shropshire, Christine mentioned Katie, whom she called the new recruit, and how she (Katie) seemed to have had a wonderful effect on Isobel. Isobel was painting again and she walked with her head held high.

Christine hadn't been down since her failure to get the job advertised in the *Guardian*. She wondered if Katie would be looking any better. She hoped so for Rufus's sake. She didn't want to cause him any undue suffering.

When they eventually arrived, Christine saw Katie and honestly thought she'd seen the ghost of Anna four years back. She was even wearing her clothes. It took her a while to collect herself.

'Katie!' she said. 'Goodness you look well.'

How Katie hated hearing those words. And anyway she didn't look well at all. She looked puffy and unhealthy. But she was fatter. And she knew that that was all they meant.

When Rufus first saw her he just gaped. But unlike the other two he didn't mince his words. 'My God, you look exactly like my sister.' And for some reason he added, 'But she wasn't half so beautiful as you are.'

Katie blushed, Isobel said '*Rufus!*' and Christine said don't be disgusting. Then there was a moment's embarrassed silence. But Rufus wouldn't take his eyes away from Katie's face. Christine thought it was time for action.

165

'Well, I don't know about anyone else, but I'd love a drink. What can I get you?'

Rufus pulled himself together and looked at his mother. 'I hear you've started painting again, Mummy. I'd love to have a look at what you've done.'

Isobel was pleased and she explained that it was entirely thanks to Katie, and that she'd been teaching her to paint as well – as part of her salary. Rufus and Isobel laughed, and they looked at Katie, so she forced a smile. But she was not happy with her salary, and she didn't like jokes being made about it.

The next morning Rufus woke up early. He heard Katie cooking bacon in the kitchen and for some reason he felt rather awkward in her company. So he didn't go straight into the kitchen. He wondered where to go and then he thought of Isobel's new paintings, so he walked into her empty studio. He saw two easels. On one was yet another passionate abstract. Rufus sighed. Try as he might, he couldn't make himself believe in his mother's form of art. He moved on to the next easel and he saw a very simple painting of a bunch of grapes. There was not a tremendous amount of talent in the picture, but it was clean and the colours were not at all aggressive. I'm not entirely sure, but I think it was when Rufus first saw Katie's painting that he fell in love with his sister all over again.

He looked at the grapes for a time and when he looked away his eye was caught by a canvas with its back to the room, standing alone in the far corner. He went over to it and turned it around.

He caught his breath and jerked backwards away from the painting. Staring right back at him was his dead sister. But he'd never seen the painting before. He looked at it more closely and, as he did so, he caught the smell of fresh paint. But there was something more immediately familiar that he couldn't put his finger on. Something about the expression in the eyes, something about the colouring. As a portrait of a young girl, Rufus could see that the painting was brilliant. But he knew it didn't quite capture his sister. There was something missing – or no, maybe there was something added. His sister never had so much fire. Just then Rufus's stomach rumbled really quite loudly and the mystery of the moment was lost. Rufus was hungry. He turned the painting back to face the wall and moved towards the kitchen. The smell of sausages was making his mouth water.

Rufus came into the kitchen just as Katie was spreading herself a fourth piece of toast. He said good morning in a well-practised easy way, and he didn't notice Katie's expression of horror at being surprised. She looked like she'd been caught with her hand in their safe. And she felt that way too.

Rufus sat down at the table and annoyingly waited to be served. But Katie was far too distracted trying to hide her toast.

I said much earlier that sex really wasn't Katie's thing. And indeed it isn't, that's all part of her wicked disease. But she has been starved of any proper male company – apart from that of the schoolmaster – for over three months, and it's no good pretending she wasn't aware of Rufus's *masculinity*.

There was electricity in the air that breakfast time.

'I've just seen your grapes,' he said.

'Oh, have you?' Katie blushed.

'There's no need to blush, I think they're wonderful. I wouldn't have mentioned them if I didn't.'

'I didn't blu- . . . well, thank you, they're not quite finished yet.' And she turned her back on him and busied herself with grilling more sausages. After a while, Katie asked Rufus if he wanted some breakfast. He took his cue and jumped up offering help. She said no, no, and he said well, then he'd love some breakfast and it was all very tense and very polite.

About half an hour later Christine came down. She said

good morning to Katie ever so graciously and then addressed all her comments to Rufus. Rufus was embarrassed by it. He was very aware of Katie's presence and he kept trying to bring her into the conversation by looking at her back, which was all of her that was visible to the room.

'I think I'll probably come back up to London with you on Sunday, Rufus, I've got one or two things I want to do,' she said.

Rufus looked apologetic. 'Oh, well, actually I was rather thinking of sticking around here a bit longer. But you don't have to, I mean you can go up for the week and then come down again on Friday.'

Christine was surprised. Usually Rufus couldn't wait to get back up to London. But she wasn't totally displeased. She was glad he was being so unselfish towards his mother. She knew he was a nice man anyway, but now she thought it proved he would be a good father.

Christine seemed to be totally oblivious of Katie's presence. She said, 'Oh, darling, it seems a shame to be separated un-necessarily when we've been so far away from each other for so long.' And then she kissed him for much longer than was called for under the circumstances. After a second or two, Rufus pushed her off and he grimaced at Katie's back. Christine looked at him and she understood the message, so she said:

'Oh don't be so neurotic, darling, Katie's part of the family, aren't you, Katie? We don't need to hide anything from her.' Then Christine laughed in an embarrassing, playful manner.

Katie kept her back firmly towards the room and pretended not to hear. Rufus reached for a cigarette and wondered if the situation had been eased.

Anyway, on Sunday night the Burtons and Katie waved Christine off from the front door and told her to drive carefully. It's an awful thing, but I'm afraid none of them was that sorry to see her go. Christine had been very vague about what it was exactly that she had to do in London. I think only Rufus knew that she was just going off blind to look for a job – any job that sounded impressive or even respectable. It was only the other day that he was going through the same thing himself and I think he should have been more supportive and sympathetic towards his girlfriend's plight. Mind you, it would have been easier if she'd admitted to him what the problem was in the first place.

That night Rufus couldn't sleep. He kept thinking of Anna, he was rehearsing the conversation that had dogged him since she'd died. He tried to reconstruct it. But he kept remembering the times he'd told her she had a fat bottom in her jodhpurs. The times he'd baited her, telling her that girls shouldn't go riding because it made their bottoms enormous. He remembered how he'd affectionately nicknamed her 'Fatso' when she first began to be noticeably thin. But she must have seen it was a joke. He couldn't forgive himself. And because of his ignorance about her illness and because he'd never really been able to understand why she'd died, and because he was basically rather a nice man, his guilt had grown disproportionate to his crime. But of course he was innocent, how could he possibly have known? He thought of Katie and he thought he wanted to pay back what he owed. He knew that Katie was alone in this world and he thought she was beautiful. She looked more and more like Anna. She *was* beautiful and I think Rufus was in love with her.

But he's in love with his sister and he's paying for her death with his guilt.

★ ★ ★

For the next five days Rufus didn't really do much. He woke up late and ate a slow, slow breakfast. He watched Katie while she cleared the kitchen, and he made easy conversation with her. He'd take the dog for a walk and stop off at the pub on the way. Come back, watch Katie eating lunch – there was something uneasy about that, he couldn't work out what it was. When Isobel and Katie disappeared to their studio after lunch, Rufus couldn't think what to do with himself. Usually he gave them half an hour and would then go and interrupt them. He'd watch them paint, but mostly he'd watch Katie.

Christine rang at about supper-time most days. Rufus always used to take the call in the kitchen, where there were plenty of people around. He wanted to play down the relationship in front of Katie. Christine was lonely in London and she told Rufus so. But he wasn't being entirely supportive and Christine noticed his coolness. She didn't say anything. Nor did she mention the job interviews for which she'd made appointments and failed to turn up. Christine was low but she was getting no support from her loved one.

On Friday Christine came home again, laden with the usual pasta from the Italian shop. While the othes were having a pre-dinner drink, she wandered into Isobel's studio. She looked at the grapes and thought 'Oh, yes, very pretty', and she looked at Isobel's disaster and sighed. She was about to walk back to the library when she too glimpsed the one painting that wasn't stacked away with the rest. It was leaning against the wall in the corner of the room with its back to the room. She turned it around and she too caught the smell of new paint. Christine saw a girl stare back at her and for a while she couldn't work out who it was. The features were so familiar, the painting was new but the girl wasn't Katie. Anna? No, not Anna. And then quite suddenly she understood. She felt a shiver run down her spine. So her plan had failed. She'd miscalculated. God, the whole thing was completely sick. She wondered if Katie had any understanding of what might be going on. She sincerely hoped not. The poor girl was muddled enough. Christine felt entirely responsible.

It was her impulse to drop the painting and charge straight into the library and have it out with Isobel there and then.

But she reasonably thought that that might do more harm than good. So she waited until the other two had gone to bed and she and Rufus were alone.

'Rufus, I know you've been down here for longer than I have, but there's something I want you to see.'

Rufus couldn't think what she was talking about, so he followed her to the studio. She went straight to the painting in the corner and turned it around. She watched Rufus's face for his reaction.

She was disappointed.

'Yes?'

'You mean you've seen it before?'

'Yes, and what's wrong with it? I think it's rather touching. I mean it's very sad, but we all of us have our own way with mourning.'

'But can't you see, Rufus? This isn't Anna, it's Katie, or rather it isn't either, I mean it's both. Can't you see the significance of this painting?'

'Oh for Christ's sake stop being so melodramatic, Christine. It's a painting of Anna, and I'd prefer it if you didn't mention your finding it to Mother. It's obviously a very private thing. If she wants us to see it then she'll show it to us in her own good time. Now come on, let's get out of here before anyone hears us. It's late. I want to go to bed.'

'Don't you understand what your mother's doing to the poor girl?'

'Shut up! Shut up! Can't you keep your fucking nose out of anything? What the bloody hell were you doing snooping around here in the first place? For the first time in her whole life my mother's actually happy – and I wouldn't be surprised if the same applied to Katie. For once in your bloody life just keep your meddling to your own affairs. Get out! Leave that painting alone and get out of this room.'

Christine watched the red face of the man she loved in amazement. The painting still leaned against her hand and she didn't move. She had forgotten all about what had brought them to the studio. Rufus had never spoken like that before. For the first time since their relationship had begun she realised that she valued him more than he her. She was seriously frightened that she might lose him, but right now any thoughts of competition hadn't entered her head. She said:

'Rufus . . . Rufus . . . you've never spoken to me like that before. I'm sorry if I offended you. Maybe I was tactless. Maybe I was wrong. I'm sorry, Rufus, please don't speak to me like that.'

Rufus's anger melted, he was no longer being threatened. But he felt no love for the pathetic copy of Christine that was standing in front of him now. He felt sorry for her, although he couldn't quite work out why. He moved forward towards her, and took the painting that was resting against her hand. He put it back in its place, with its face against the wall. Then he put his arm around his girlfriend and led her out of the room. Christine was crying. I think it was from shock.

Rufus didn't say a word as he led her upstairs. They both undressed in silence apart from the occasional sniff from Christine and then they both pretended to sleep. When at last she did sleep, Christine dreamed of the babies that she yearned for. And neither of them ever mentioned the episode again.

★　　★　　★

Rufus's job began on Monday, so he and Christine travelled back up to London on Sunday night. The house seemed quite empty without them. Katie missed Rufus, and she spent the rest of that evening fantasising about living with him happily ever afterwards.

The week in London was very tense for both Christine and Rufus. Ever since Friday night poor Christine had been on her best behaviour.

Now that Rufus was back, their social life awoke with a

vengeance. They went out every night. And they made only one miserable attempt at love-making which only served to remind Christine how desperate her situation was. She didn't want to lose him.

On Wednesday Christine told Rufus that she'd arranged for them to go and stay the weekend with some friends up in Yorkshire and for some reason it made Rufus absolutely furious. How dared she make arrangements with his time without even consulting him. Anyone would think she owned him. They weren't *married* for God's sake.

Now that was mean. They had been as good as married for the last four years. And for the last four years she had always accepted invitations on his behalf if they sounded like fun. And the people in Yorkshire were his friends more than hers. Anyway, Rufus refused to go. He said he'd already made arrangements to go down to Shropshire this weekend, and seeing as he was the one who was working then he didn't see why he couldn't make his own decisions about what to do with his limited free time.

Christine's patience and her good behaviour suddenly wore out.

'Oh for Christ's sake, Rufus, stop behaving like a pig. What on earth has got into you? You were obviously spoilt on your silly little jaunt. Well, it's up to you. *I'm* going to spend the weekend in Yorkshire, you can go where you bloody well want.'

So Rufus, like a defiant, self-righteous teenager, said, 'Right. I'm going to Shropshire.'

And that's exactly what they did.

CHAPTER 12

Isobel Was Surprised and delighted when she heard that Rufus was not only coming down again this weekend but that he was coming alone. When she heard the taxi draw up outside the front door she ran towards it. And she greeted her son as though he'd just come back from fighting in the war. Katie hung back and waited for Rufus to spot her, which didn't take too long. He disentangled himself from his mother's arms and took three perfect Mills and Boon strides towards his waif. He rested his strong hands on her delicate shoulders and he gazed long and hard into her beautiful, moistened eyes.

'Katie . . .' he said, 'even more beautiful . . .'

And good Katie dropped her eyes to the floor like any modest maiden should.

Meanwhile Isobel had wandered off in the direction of the library, calling half-heartedly for the dog. She thought it was probably about time it was put out, or it'd made a mess in one of the guests' bedrooms.

Rufus said, 'I love you, Katie.'

And Katie said, 'I love you, too.'

Then Isobel came back. She didn't seem to be at all aware of what was going on.

'Have either of you seen the dog?'

They leapt apart.

Rufus said, 'Er, no, I don't think so, perhaps it's outside.'

'Well, never mind. Do let's stop hanging around in this freezing cold hall. Who wants what to drink?'

Isobel handed Katie a gin and tonic. She said, 'It's lovely now, we're all one big happy family again.'

Katie felt like an intruder, and she was very ill at ease. Had Rufus been joking? What about Christine? He must have been joking. She didn't dare look up from the carpet all evening.

Rufus kept up his easy patter throughout dinner. He told them about his new job. He and Isobel did most of the talking. In fact, I don't think Katie volunteered one single comment. And now she genuinely didn't feel hungry. She pushed her food around her plate but she couldn't force any down her throat. She prayed that Isobel wouldn't notice, and more importantly, that she wouldn't comment on it. But Isobel did both.

'Oh, Katie darling, don't say you're up to your old tricks again. Please eat what's on your plate, it's hardly a very big helping.'

Rufus looked up, alarmed. 'What old tricks?'

'Nothing, I'm just not hungry.' Katie thought she might be going to cry.

'Katie had a little problem which we're all fighting to get her over, and she's doing so well.'

Katie gave Isobel the meanest look she could muster. 'Would you mind not talking about me as if I wasn't in the room?'

Isobel realised she might have been a bit tactless and she blushed.

Rufus thought he understood the little problem and he supposed he wasn't that surprised. He didn't say anything, somehow it seemed quite fitting.

Immediately after supper Isobel said she was tired and that she wanted to go to bed. Katie was tempted to run away too. But apart from anything else someone had to clear up the remnants of their meal.

'I'll leave you young people to it,' Isobel said. And Rufus said he thought that was probably a very good idea.

Rufus watched Katie wash up in silence. He sat back in his chair and smoked a cigarette. Very masculine, very attractive. *I* think he should have offered to help, and if it had been anyone else, so would Katie.

When she'd finished, Rufus said, 'Did you mean what you said in the hall?'

'Did you?'

'I did.'

'And so did I. What about Christine?'

'What about her? We're finished and she knows it. Our relationship isn't leading anywhere. We both know it's come to an end.' And as he said so he felt a twinge of guilt. It sounded very callous. He even felt a certain sadness. They'd had some good times together.

In Yorkshire, Christine was sitting with her host and hostess and another couple. They were all old friends. It was after dinner and they were all quite stoned. Four of them were giggling about John Travolta's sore bottom because of the label in his underpants. But Christine couldn't find it funny. At first she tried quite hard to laugh, but her thoughts kept returning to Rufus. What was up with him these days? And why did he suddenly want to spend all his time in Shropshire? Then she thought of Katie. Then she remembered the scene about the painting in the studio and at last she understood. Out loud she said:

'Wow, but have I miscalculated!'

Then one of the guests turned towards her and said, 'Wow, but have you got a sore bottom!' and the other three collapsed into still more offensive laughter.

Christine said, 'I'm going upstairs to pack. I think I've made an awful lot of mistakes. I've got to get down to Shropshire first thing in the morning.'

Her host stood up and tried to make polite conversation with her about her miscalculations. Eventually, Christine was able to escape.

In Shropshire, Rufus stubbed out his cigarette and pushed back his chair. He moved over to Katie who was still standing at the kitchen sink. He took her in his arms and pushed her face into his chest. For a while he stroked her hair and poor Katie, who was sadly out of practice, didn't know what to do with her feet. Then Rufus put his hand beneath her chin and pushed her face up in his direction. He kissed her and she smelt the cigarette on his breath.

Katie felt no great sexual stirring, but she felt strangely comforted. She wanted to show him her sympathy and her gratitude towards his family. And she was unused to being loved – or wanted – or desired.

He pushed his crotch into Katie's stomach. His hand moved down towards her breast and when he found it – or what was left of it – pictures of shaved pubic hairs and balding heads and swollen, vomit-sore glands flashed through his mind. He heard Christine's monotonous voice. 'In particularly bad cases of anorexia victims have been known to lacerate their own genitalia . . .' Rufus pushed Katie away from him and groaned. He wasn't sure if he could go through with it. He wanted to clear his mind. He looked at Katie and he realised he couldn't back out now.

'Come on,' he said, 'let's go to bed.'

They walked up the stairs towards Rufus and Christine's room in silence. They didn't want to wake up Isobel.

In Yorkshire, Christine was packing her bags with an uncanny amount of urgency. She kept thinking of the portrait, and of Katie in Anna's clothes.

In Shropshire, Isobel found she couldn't sleep. She didn't smoke and she didn't read. She decided now was the time to tidy her room.

Rufus saw the body. He saw Katie's body, he saw Anna's body. He saw a grotesque, distorted, shrivelled body. But she was beautiful, he couldn't back out now.

Isobel started with her clothes chest. She opened the bottom drawer and she saw the diary.

Christine sat on the edge of her bed and lit a cigarette. She thought of them in Shropshire. She thought of them fucking.

Rufus led Katie to the bed.
    They fucked.
    It hurt.

Isobel opened the diary and she read, 'Most of all I love Rufus, but I hate them all. I think I'm going to die.' It was the last page, written about a week before she was taken to the hospital. It meant nothing to Isobel. She didn't die. Isobel threw the diary out.

Christine thought he'd ask Katie to marry him. She was sure she'd say yes. Katie was so lonely.

Rufus was about to come. He asked Katie to marry him. She said yes. He came.

They talked about the future and then she crept back to her room. Hours later, all four of them were asleep.

★   ★   ★

Katie was up to cook breakfast at the usual time the next morning. Rufus had already left for Shrewsbury. He left a letter under Katie's bedroom door. He was charging on blindly to buy her an engagement ring. She wasn't to mention a word of it to his mother until he returned.

At nine Isobel came downstairs, and far from telling her all about it, Katie couldn't look her in the face. Isobel wondered what was troubling her but preferred to pretend she'd noticed nothing amiss. She said she'd be in her studio until Rufus came back and Katie felt relieved. Rufus was expected back at about lunch-time.

Christine couldn't get anyone to drop her at the station until ten. That meant she wouldn't reach the Rectory until lunch-time. She felt a little calmer now, and as the train sped towards what she regarded as her home, she wondered if she wasn't being a little hysterical.

At half-past twelve, Isobel decided she wanted a break from her painting. She called Katie down from her bedroom and asked her to come and have a drink. Katie couldn't think of any reasonable excuse to get herself out of it. So she came downstairs. Isobel talked about her progress in the studio that morning and Katie swigged at her gin and tonic.

Christine's train stopped at Shrewsbury, and she hailed a taxi to take her to the Rectory. Ten minutes later she was turning into the Rectory's drive.

At the same time Katie heard the front door slam. She jumped up and a couple of seconds later Rufus walked into the room victorious.

Christine's taxi drew up and she fumbled for the right change. She pushed the front door open.

'Mother, I've got something rather surprising to tell you.' He paused, he was fumbling in all his pockets looking for the ring.

Christine walked into the hall and heard noises coming from the library. The library door was wide open; she walked straight towards it and paused at the threshold. How was she going to justify her sudden appearance like this? Rufus would think she was spying on him.

'Katie and I are engaged to be married.'

'Darling!' said Isobel. What surprising, what wonderful news! She moved towards him with her arms outstretched to embrace him.

Katie saw Christine. 'Rufus!' She stared and Rufus turned in the direction of her stare. He froze.

Christine was in control. 'Did I hear you correctly?'

'I . . .'

'You did.' Isobel was *gloating*.

Christine ignored her. 'Did I hear you correctly, Rufus?'

'I'm sorry, Christine, I never meant it to work out like this.'

'You bastard.'

Isobel laughed a mad, hysterical laugh. 'But you can't call my son a bastard, he's getting married. We're all one big happy family again.'

'Keep out of this, Mother. This is between me and Christine.'

'Oh but it isn't!' Christine lost her control. 'But it isn't between me and you at all. Can't you see what you're doing? This isn't *my* problem, Rufus, it's yours,' she turned to Isobel, 'and yours,' and to Katie, 'and, poor, pathetic waif, it's yours too now.' She turned towards Rufus. 'You see her? Do you see her? What's she called, Rufus? What's she called? Katie, do they ever call you Anna? Do they?' Christine was screaming now, and the silence while she waited for Katie's reply was probably more shocking to the listeners than what they refused to hear.

'No.'

'Don't they? *Never?* But you see they don't think of you as Katie. They think you're Anna. Do you remember? Rufus's dead baby sister. Isobel's dead baby daughter. They never really knew her and they can't forgive themselves. But now she's been resurrected. Are you following me, Katie?'

Katie turned away. 'I don't want to hear any more of this.'

'That's because it's the truth. People never like hearing the truth. And this is an ugly truth' – she turned to Rufus – 'isn't it, darling? You could never really forgive yourself, could you, darling? Well, this is one hell of a perverted way to mourn.'

'Oh for Christ's sake, Christine, stop it. You're hysterical.'

'No, darling,' said Isobel, 'she's just jealous. Tell her to get out of here. Get her out.'

'All right then, to hell with you all. I'm leaving. And you, Rufus, you, go on then, fuck your stick insect, fuck your resurrected anorexic baby sister. And God bless you. But you'll never bring her back to life, and you'll never salve your conscience. Anna's dead. Learn to live with it. DEAD, DEAD, DEAD. And we were all responsible. All of us. Don't you ever forget it.'

Christine left. Later she would be sending them lawyers' letters to reclaim the very large sum of money she had lent them to do up the hotel. But now it was only mad Isobel who was practical enough to think of finances. The scene quite clearly hadn't shaken her at all.

'Oh dear, oh dear, how are we ever going to pay back all that money we owe her?'

Rufus looked shaken and pale beneath his oriental sunburn. He might have gone over to his fiancée who was crying on the sofa, but right now he was thinking about his own problems. He never knew Christine could be so excitable. He must have underestimated how much she loved him.

Isobel was the first to notice Katie crying. She said, 'Come along, darling, you mustn't let these little scenes upset you. I think this all calls for a bottle of champagne. Rufus, you were about to give Katie a ring, as I remember.'

Katie was still crying when Isobel picked up her left hand and pulled it towards Rufus. She didn't look up when Rufus slid the ring on her finger. And when Isobel let go of her hand it dropped limply back on to her lap. She didn't look at the ring.

'Do cheer up, darling, this is supposed to be the happiest day in a girl's life,' said Isobel.

And at last Katie looked up. She saw the sweet look of concern on her fiancé's face and she smiled. But of course this was the happiest day of her life. She loved them and they loved her. What was the problem?

'That's better,' said Isobel. 'Now, before Rufus goes down to the cellar, I'd like to present you with a little pre-wedding gift. Wait there.' And she skipped away out of the room.

Rufus and Katie didn't speak during the minute and a half that Isobel was away, nor did they even look at each other.

Isobel came in struggling under the bulk of her canvas. She turned it around.

'A portrait of your pretty little wife.' She grinned.

Katie acted first. 'Oh that's lovely, Mrs Burton.' She got up from the sofa and kissed her on the cheek. 'Thank you very much.'

And Rufus had time to compose himself and to block out any uncomfortable thoughts and memories.

'Thank you, Mother. It's beautiful. But I promise it doesn't nearly do her justice, what artist could?' He looked across at his future bride, fresh from school and new to the city, and she smiled so warmly up at him. He smiled back. Christine was insane.

And so Rufus and Katie were married. Maybe Katie's health improved, maybe she was even able to have children. Maybe they lived happily ever after, but I doubt it.